ONCE
UPON A
BUGGY

Also in The Amish of Apple Creek series

Happily Ever Amish

And read more Shelley Shepard Gray in

Amish Christmas Twins
An Amish Second Christmas
Christmas at the Amish Bakeshop
An Amish Christmas Star

SHELLEY SHEPARD GRAY

ONCE UPON A BUGGY

KENSINGTON
PUBLISHING CORP.

www.kensingtonbooks.com

KENSINGTON BOOKS are published by

Kensington Publishing Corp.
119 West 40th Street
New York, NY 10018

All Kensington titles, imprints, and distributed lines are available at special quantity discounts for bulk purchases for sales promotion, premiums, fund-raising, educational, or institutional use. Special book excerpts or customized printings can also be created to fit specific needs. For details, write or phone the office of the Kensington Special Sales Manager: Attn. Special Sales Department. Kensington Publishing Corp, 119 West 40th Street, New York, NY 10018. Phone: 1-800-221-2647.

Library of Congress Control Number: 2022948722

The K with book logo Reg. US Pat & TM Off.

ISBN: 978-1-4967-3983-4
First Kensington Hardcover Edition: April 2023

ISBN: 978-1-4967-3986-5 (trade)

ISBN: 978-1-4967-3989-6 (ebook)

10 9 8 7 6 5 4 3 2 1

Printed in the United States of America

Always be humble and gentle. Be patient with each other, making allowance for each other's faults because of your love.

—Ephesians 4:2

To receive the full value of joy, you must have someone to divide it with.

—Amish proverb

Prologue

The smoke from the flames was so thick, May Schott could barely see more than a few inches in front of her face. The choking clouds hung in the air, practically singeing her skin.

Holding her in place.

At least, that was what it felt like. Even though her mind was screaming for her to run toward the open barn door, the rest of her body didn't seem to be cooperating. Her limbs felt heavy, and her eyes stung and watered. She was paralyzed.

Attempting to take a fortifying breath, she coughed. It was beginning to feel like the fire had taken all the oxygen in the building. Maybe it had.

Run! a voice inside of her called out. Unfortunately, for some reason, the rest of her didn't think that was a good idea.

May jumped as a flame-covered beam crashed to the ground, sending sparks flying into the air. They looked like bright fireflies, cutting through the thick smoke.

They were almost beautiful.

"May!"

Carl was calling her. Nee, he was yelling. His expression was fierce, his voice urgent. "May! May, don'tcha hear me?" Reaching for her hand, he tugged. "Come on! The rest of the barn is about to ignite!"

She wanted to move. She really did. But the only thing that seemed to make any sense was her certainty that in order to get out of the barn, they were going to have to walk right next to the fire. It was so close, less than two feet away.

The flames were going to be so hot. They'd singe her dress. Burn her skin.

He pulled on her arm again. "May! We have to get out."

There was some part of her head—or maybe it was her heart?—that knew her best friend was right. Of course, it was her fault they were in the barn in the first place. She'd had a crush on Carl Hilty her whole life. It was only recently that he'd begun to return her interest. They'd been flirting at singings and such, but she wanted more from him.

Now that she was sixteen and he was seventeen, she wanted him to start courting her.

No, she wanted him to be her boyfriend.

So she'd decided to push things a bit. She'd asked him to meet her in the feed barn on the edge of her family's property. No one would know where they were. They could finally talk for a while without having her younger brother or his younger siblings disturb them.

Even though it had been windy and a storm had threatened, he'd met her there. When he'd stared at her in the dim light, there had been a new awareness between them. She'd sensed that he was tired of biding his time as well.

At first, they'd just talked. Then Carl had moved closer. And then finally . . . after years and years of flirting and circling around each other, he'd kissed her. That first kiss had been everything she'd ever dreamed of. Everything she'd ever yearned for.

With his arms around her, May had been sure that everything was going to change between them. It was all going to be so different. So much better. All the girls in Apple Creek would know that handsome Carl Hilty was off the market—because he was hers. She'd felt attractive and triumphant and giddy.

And then a crash of thunder cracked over their heads.

The barn had caught fire.

"May, come on!" Carl pulled again. Bringing her back to the present.

"I can't." She couldn't stop staring at the flames. At the way they were devouring everything in their path.

"You have to. We're going to burn up. Move!" He tugged again.

She blinked. The flames had grown even higher. The glowing combination of red and orange held her mesmerized. She couldn't seem to look away. Already her skin felt scorched.

Carl's arm wrapped around her waist. "I'd carry you if I could, but it's too far, and there's too much debris on the ground. I might stumble." Panic laced his tone. "May . . . May, I know you're scared, but you've got to help me. There's no other way out."

Finally, finally, it hit her. Her hesitation was putting him in harm's way. "Okay . . . But—"

"*Nee*, we're not talking right now. All we're going to do is run. Come on!" He reached for her hand again. "In a minute, we could be outside in the cool air. We'll be safe. Just a minute. You can do that, jah?"

She nodded.

"Now, run!"

Galvanized by his will, she did as he asked. She clung to his hand with one hand, grabbed the hem of her dress with the other, and ran toward the exit.

The flames were hot. The scent of burning wood, mixed

with something dark and dusty, enveloped her. And the noise! It surrounded her. Filled her ears.

"Faster, May!"

She pushed forward. Her skin felt sunburned, sensitive. Tears filled her eyes. She didn't know if she'd ever been so scared.

And then she tripped.

Landing on a piece of burning wood, she screamed in terror. Carl stopped, turned around, and pulled her to her feet. His arms around her, he pushed her forward, shielding her from the worst of the flames.

Seconds later, she was out. "May! Praise the Lord!" exclaimed a stranger's voice.

The man picked her up and carried her to safety. Lying on the ground, she gasped. "Carl!"

"Hush now, don't talk."

"*Nee.*" She tried again. Tried to tell them about Carl. That he was surely hurt. "He—" But her explanation was interrupted by another round of coughing. It continued painfully as she tried to breathe. Her lungs felt seared.

"May, please, please calm down. Help is on the way! I see the lights of the fire trucks in the distance." It was her mother's voice now.

"But Carl! I need to find Carl!"

"He's out, too," another voice said. It sounded flat, though. Not encouraging at all.

Even though her eyelashes felt singed, she opened her eyes and tried to find the speaker. "Is he all right?" she whispered.

"I don't know," the speaker said.

She gaped as the area was lit up with red and blue lights, and sirens filled the air. Smoke and flames cast a hellish glow over the scene. At least thirty people had gathered around the barn.

But she couldn't find Carl.

"Ma'am?" an authoritative voice called out. "I heard your daughter is here? Is that correct?"

"*Jah*. I mean, yes."

"What is her name?"

"May Schott. I mean, this here is May."

Two firemen knelt down beside her. At least, she thought they were firemen.

"I'm Doug, Miss. You're going to be okay." A mask was put over her face. "This is oxygen. Slow breaths, now, okay?" he soothed.

She did as he asked, only vaguely aware of her hand being poked.

All she heard was the roar of the flames, the low murmur of the crowd, and the frantic call for Life Flight. Carl's pleading, begging her to move so they'd get to safety.

That's when she realized that Carl was not okay at all . . . and his condition was all her fault.

Chapter 1

Six Years Later
April

May didn't know everything, but she did know one thing for sure and for certain: Her mother had been wrong. Some dreams really did come true—the ones that counted, anyway. After years of wishing and hoping and praying, Carl Hilty had come back home. Her next-door neighbor, childhood best friend—the boy who'd saved her life—had finally returned. She was going to be able to see him in person.

Adrenaline, fueled by a surge of nervousness and excitement, shot through her as she craned her neck. She was anxious to catch even a glimpse of Carl, but it was next to impossible. It looked as if the entire Amish population of Apple Creek was currently trying to do the same thing.

May supposed she shouldn't have been surprised. Carl was a hero, and he'd been gone for such a very long time. Six years was practically an eternity.

"Do you see him, May?" Camille asked.

Turning to her girlfriend, pretty, demure Camille, May shook her head. "*Nee.* I wish I was taller."

Camille chuckled. "If I had a dime for every time you've said those words, I'd be a rich woman."

"I know." Frustrated by the crowd—as well as their position at the back of it—she rose on her tiptoes. "I know there's nothing I can do about my height. I'm just anxious."

"Don't worry so much. I'm sure Carl's trying to find his way to you."

"I hope so." But maybe not? Unconsciously, she rubbed her thigh. She could feel the ridged, four-inch scar under the fabric. It hardly hurt at all anymore.

Seconds passed. Some of the men who must have greeted Carl first walked away. Little by little, the crowd began to thin.

"I bet you could make your way to the front now," Camille said. "I'm pretty sure I see Able Hilty up there."

Carl's *daed*. Picturing the somber man who always avoided looking her way, May swallowed hard. The nervousness she'd been attempting to keep at bay surged again. "I'm sure Mr. Hilty wouldn't appreciate me appearing in the middle of Carl's homecoming. I'll wait right here."

Actually, she was starting to think that this moment wasn't the right time or place for her and Carl to renew their friendship. It might be the absolute worst spot.

It was, after all, a mighty big event. Most everyone in their church district was gathered together for an Easter egg hunt and picnic in the Millers' back field. Easter was just around the corner, and with it had come some welcome sunny weather. Everyone was eager to see each other after weeks and weeks of snow and cold. So it was a joyous day, and one made better by Carl's return.

But perhaps it wasn't the best place to hug Carl? Maybe not the right time to clutch his hands, the way she used to do, and share just how grateful she was for his bravery?

Or share how much she'd missed him.

Camille stepped to the left. "I heard he's wearing a Guardians baseball cap. Do you think that's true?"

"I don't know. Maybe?" Carl had gone up to Cleveland for treatment at the burn unit and had ended up staying. Though she'd heard a rumor that he'd elected not to be baptized, she didn't know if that was true or not.

It was yet another sign that, although she'd missed him so much, Carl might not have felt the same way. No, it was a given that he didn't feel the same way. But who could blame him?

She was the reason he'd been hurt.

Camille, oblivious to her dark thoughts, was still moving about, trying her best to sneak a peek at Carl. "Ack! This is so frustrating."

May hid a smile. Camille's complaint was as unexpected as it was true. "It is frustrating, but you're right. I've waited for six years; I can wait a little while longer."

"I'm impressed." Camille's brown eyes studied her more carefully. "You're usually a lot more eager to be in the thick of things."

She used to be. After the fire, though? She'd tried hard to curb her desires. "I'll see him in time." Whenever Carl wanted to see her. No, whenever the Lord was ready for them to be reunited. Yes, that's what she needed to reflect upon. The Lord had a hand in her and Carl's lives. She needed to abide by His wishes.

Camille was prevented from replying when another one of their friends approached. Soon, they were talking like magpies together.

Glad that she had a little more time to prepare herself, May leaned against the metal wall of the Millers' new barn. A lot of people had metal barns these days—the metal was cheaper to obtain than lumber; it went up more easily and with less manpower. But on days like today, in the begin-

ning middle of April? Well, it seemed like a shame. Leaning
up against the cool steel didn't feel the same as a weathered
barn, she mused. There was just something about the mel-
lowness of wood that was worn and faded from years of use.

Realizing the direction her mind had gone, she jerked upright. How could she ever think such a thing? That wooden
barn had been the reason for everything that had happened.
And just like that, she could smell the smoke and could feel
the chill in the air—and remembered how dark the barn had
been that evening—right up until the time it had erupted in
flames.

The noise had been so loud. The heat unbearable. She'd
been scared and stunned until Carl had pulled on her hand.

He'd been yelling at her. Yelling for her to hurry. No,
begging her to move. When she'd finally done as he'd asked
and had run by his side, she tripped.

Then she'd started screaming in terror.

Remembering the way the flames had touched her skin,
how it had felt like a thousand needles, she swayed. Sweat
formed on her brow when she recalled how Carl had placed
himself between her and the worst of the fire.

May blinked as she tried to push away the memories. Just
as she did in the middle of the night. Just like she had almost
every night for the last six years.

"May?"

She shook her head. Too afraid to move. "I . . ."

"Hey, May? Are you okay?"

She jerked upright. Blinked at the blinding sun. And at
Camille's concerned expression. "Do you need something?
Some water, maybe?"

Camille was talking about a glass of water. Because she
was standing in the sun. Pushing herself back into the present, she shook her head. "*Nee.* I'm sorry. I . . . I was just
thinking about something."

"Hey, what are you doing? You don't need to hide things from me, May." Camille grabbed her fingers and intertwined them with her own. "Are you scared to see him? Are you afraid to see Carl again?"

"Of course not." It was a lie, clearly. She had many reasons to be afraid to see him.

Camille lowered her voice. "Listen, Emma just told me that you might want to prepare yourself. She said Carl looks a sight different."

"I've heard that, too." No one would expect otherwise. Carl had sustained burns over half his body. His burns were so bad that he'd been sent to the Shriners Hospital in Dayton so his family wouldn't have to worry about the price of his surgeries and medical care. Eventually, he'd moved to the Cleveland Clinic for more care. Carl Hilty had suffered through several more surgeries, skin grafts, and rehabilitations there.

She'd stopped hearing about them after he'd gotten through four.

No, that wasn't right. She'd stopped being able to listen after the fourth. Especially since he'd refused her offers to visit, just as he'd refused to take her calls after that one time.

Maybe it had been guilt or the need to sleep at night — or maybe she'd finally gotten it through her head that Carl didn't want to hear from her ever again.

Whatever the reason, May had stopped expecting replies to her letters after his fourth surgery. She'd stopped writing to him after his fifth. It had hurt her heart too much.

She'd always suspected that her heart had been rather weak.

Hating the direction her thoughts were going, May scanned the area, anxious to find something — no, anything — to help divert her mind from the dark path on which it was headed. Looking down at her boots, she spied a tiny frog on the soft mud next to the metal barn. She knelt down and gave it a little nudge. The metal was cool now, but the day was supposed to get warm. By noon, the metal walls would be hot to the touch and the ground hard and solid. Neither would be very tiny frog friendly.

Careful not to hurt it, she nudged it with the tip of a finger. "Get on your way now, frog," she murmured. "Hop on over to the field. I know there's critters there, but you'll likely have a better chance of surviving. Ain't so?"

"Hey, May?"

The frog had hopped three times, then stopped again. "Just a sec, Camille. I'm waiting to see—"

"May, stand up," she interrupted. "Stand up now."

Startled, May did as Camille asked.

And came face to face with Carl himself.

Carl was tall now. Easily almost six feet. His eyes were just as beautiful as she remembered—a myriad of blues and greens. She'd used to tell him that such pretty eyes were wasted on a boy.

But almost everything else about him was different. The pain haunting those eyes. The scars on his face. And on his neck. And covering his right hand.

The way he was staring at her as if he didn't know who she was. That had to be a mistake, though. Right?

They'd been too close for him to have forgotten her. Hadn't they?

Or had she felt so bad about the break in their relationship that she'd turned it into something more than it was?

Unconsciously, she rubbed the ridge on her thigh again. His eyes followed. May could practically feel the entire population of Apple Creek watching them. Waiting for her to launch herself into Carl's arms. For her to cry happy tears because they were reunited at last.

Maybe he felt the stares, too, because at last he met her eyes. "May."

Overcome with emotion, she felt her bottom lip tremble. "Carl," she whispered. "You're back. I'm so glad you came back to Apple Creek."

Somehow looking even more pained, the boy she'd once loved so much studied her for another long second. Then, without another word, he turned and walked away.

After six years, Carl Hilty had seen her, then walked away without saying anything more than her name.

He must hate her now. People started whispering. A low buzz surrounded her, sounding as if she was surrounded by a swarm of bees. Each one gossiping, talking, no doubt ready to sting her with an unkind comment.

Well, any jabs she received would be no more than she deserved. Her lungs tightened. She shouldn't have expected anything else. After all, he might have saved her, but she was the reason they'd been in that barn in the first place. Closing her eyes, she ignored Camille, who was reaching out for her hand. Instead, she turned and pressed her forehead to the side of the barn and tried her best to think only of how cool the metal felt against her skin.

Instead, she was reminded of how hot the burning wood had been in another barn on another day. How it had scorched her leg for that split second.

All before Carl had dragged her to safety. Just seconds before the burning embers had fallen on him and changed both of their lives forever.

Chapter 2

He'd survived more surgeries than he cared to count, more pain than he'd imagined was possible, and likely had spent more hours completely by himself than anyone in Apple Creek.

Because of all that, Carl didn't feel normal. Or that he fit in. Worse, he wasn't even sure whether he wanted to fit in. Pretty much everyone had been staring at him as if he was some kind of deformed beast.

But, of course, that wasn't fair. He knew what he looked like, and it wasn't pretty. Three years ago, counselors had started visiting him once a week. At first, he'd resented their help and hadn't been receptive to their suggestions. But in spite of his best attempts to ignore their advice, he'd slowly begun to take it.

His anxiety eased, and his doubts became more manageable. A woman named Hilda had been particularly persistent. She'd talked with him for hours about how he needed to come to terms with the fact that sometimes a person wasn't being rude when they took a long look at him. It was just that shock of his scars made one take a second and third glance.

It was understandable.

Unfortunately, when that happened, his brain understood, but his heart couldn't seem to keep up.

"Want to get out of here?" Kevin asked.

Surprised, he turned to his sixteen-year-old brother. "How are we going to manage that? Mamm and Daed are here."

"I know, but they'll understand if we dart out. They probably won't even notice."

"Of course, they're going to notice, Kevin. They aren't going to be okay with me leaving early, either. This is my coming home party."

"Whatever. If they object, then Ally and I will run interference."

His brother and sister were the best people he knew. From the moment he'd been airlifted from Apple Creek, they'd never wavered in making sure his needs were met first. He had an idea he would never know the hardships they had endured at the farm while he'd been sitting in a hospital bed.

"You know I can take care of myself, right? I'm not only twenty-five years old, but I've also been on my own for years."

"Just because you have a fancy English job and ain't Amish no longer doesn't mean you aren't my brother." Standing up straighter, Kevin added, "And just because I'm younger, it don't mean that I'm not right."

Carl knew better than to argue further. It didn't matter if Kevin was sixteen or six. Whenever his brother adopted that tone in his voice, there was no stopping him. "Then, *jah*, fine. Let's get out of here."

Kevin grinned. "Whew. I thought for a minute that you were going to want to stay."

"Wait a minute, running away isn't just for my benefit, is it? You were ready to leave, too, right?"

"Of course, I was. You know how much I hate it when all the folks try to pretend that you're not there."

"It's normal to not know how to react to the way I look."

"Maybe. Maybe not."

"Kevin, not everyone stares because they're rude. I've come to accept that."

"Hmm. I hope that was May's excuse."

"Don't worry about May."

"Why not?" Kevin stopped walking toward the end of the driveway and stared at him. " She was standing right in front of you. Said your name." Looking at him more intently, he added, "And you said hers."

"It didn't mean anything." Realizing that his excuse sounded as flimsy as it was, he added, "I wasn't even positive it was May. It's been a long time since I was home."

Kevin's brows pulled together. "I didn't think it had been that long, but no worries. "In any case, I'd be surprised if it hadn't taken you a moment to recognize her. She's a beauty now, no doubt about that. Back when you two used to play together, she was just a freckle-faced nuisance."

"Her hair is darker now."

Kevin nodded. "It's brown. Rich brown, like the color of walnuts in the fall. Her skin is real pretty, too. She's the only woman I've ever seen look fetching with so many freckles."

"She's changed a lot."

"*Jah*. Pretty much the only thing that didn't change is her height. She's still only a little over five feet." Slapping him on the back, Kevin added, "Don't worry. I'm sure the next time you see her, you'll recognize her right off the bat."

He nodded. Of course, he was lying. The truth was that

he had noticed her practically the moment she'd arrived. How could he not? She'd been the prettiest girl there. He'd stared at her, but when her eyes had widened, he'd looked away, embarrassed to be caught gazing at her like a besotted fool.

Then, something that his brother had said snagged his attention. Skin really pretty?

"Kevin, do you like her?"

His brother flushed. "Of course, I don't."

His brother might only be sixteen, but that didn't mean he couldn't admire a pretty girl. "It's okay if you do. You don't need to keep it a secret or anything." Of course, every single bit of that statement had been another lie, but what difference did it make? He owed his brother everything. If Kevin and May liked each other, Carl would honor their relationship. No, he would support and encourage it.

His brother's frown deepened. "Carl, I just said we aren't courting. What's gotten into you?" He rested a hand on his arm. "And why would you ever say it doesn't make any difference if I'm seeing May or not? She was your girl."

"She was my friend. Six years ago."

"*Nee*, she was your friend since birth. Mamm and Daed used to say that the Lord made you two neighbors because He believed you were meant to know each other."

Carl remembered his parents saying that. More important, he remembered that he used to think the same thing himself. Just thinking about his childhood naïveté made him embarrassed. How could he have ever been so full of himself as to believe that the Lord had nothing better to do than watch over May and him?

"I don't want to talk about her and me."

Kevin opened his mouth but seemed to think better of objecting at the last minute. "Fine, but I don't like it."

Any further fussing was stalled by their sister's approach.

Ally was blond, had brown eyes, and was very fit. She was easily the most athletic of the three siblings. When they were younger, she'd always been the one to set up a kickball or volleyball game. He and Kevin had even teased her that she only went to Pinecraft in February in order to play beach volleyball.

She still went walking or running or rode her bike as often as she could. It was obvious to see that she was in good shape, even though she wore a loose-fitting, short-sleeved blue dress.

She practically loped forward, her eyes intent on her brothers. "What are you two doing? Mamm and Daed are looking for ya."

"We were thinking about sneaking out of here."

"Really?" Her voice filled with compassion. "Is this reunion too much for you, Carl?"

"Not really. Kevin and I were just thinking about it."

"I said you'd cover for us," Kevin added.

"I will, if you need me to . . . but I'd rather not, if you don't mind. Mamm and Daed were so excited this morning. They were looking forward to spending time with all three of their *kinner*. It's not too much to ask, is it?"

"*Nee*. Why don't you take me around, Ally? Half the problem is that I don't remember everyone's names. A couple of people went so far as to ask me if I remembered their names." Remembering the crestfallen expressions, he added, "Trust me, every time I said no, it brought up ill feelings."

"More like hurt feelings, *jah*?"

"Maybe . . . maybe not."

She held out her hand. "Come with me. I'll make sure I say everyone's names, and we'll get through it together."

"You don't have to do this, Carl," Kevin said.

"I know, but it's not going to get easier. Besides, the worst part is over."

Ally smiled. "You're right. You got here and showed up for the first time since the accident. And you survived."

Carl nodded, but he knew that the part he'd been dreading most was seeing May again. Now that the first meeting was over, he could dodge her for a while longer.

Until he returned to Cleveland and went back to his life. He tried not to think about how easy it was to live in isolation in the city.

Or how lonely.

Chapter 3

Ally met Walker in "their" spot later that night. About seven months ago, when things between them had begun to heat up, they'd found a little cove near the Millers' lake. The lake was barely more than a large pond and was ignored by the Millers, for the most part. Since it was about a ten-minute walk from both of their houses, she and Walker had agreed it was the perfect meeting place.

Since it was only mid-May, the temperature was still cool at night. Ally had put on warm stockings and wore a soft, wheat-colored alpaca cardigan over her dress. To this day, her mother still didn't realize that the soft yarn Ally had used came from the Schotts' alpacas.

Just as if they hadn't seen each other in weeks, Ally hugged Walker hello. After kissing her brow, he guided her to the thick quilt he'd spread on the ground. Sitting next to him, snuggled against his side, was the best part of her day.

It always was.

"So, that went horribly," Ally said to Walker later that night.

Walker frowned. "Do you really think so? I thought it went well enough. May didn't say one word about Carl when we were driving home in the buggy."

"Of course your sister wasn't going to say a word to you or your parents."

"Come on."

"Your parents are your parents, and you . . ."

"Yes?"

She almost giggled. He was actually looking offended that Ally might think he was a typical boy. She nudged him with her toe. "Walker, you're her younger brother. Sisters don't confide dark secrets to their younger brothers."

"You might not, but May and I are different. I promise, she knows I love her—and that I would've listened to whatever she wanted to say about Carl."

"I know you would have, but she probably still would've been afraid to say something to you."

"Because . . ."

"Because everyone knows that your parents don't want her to have anything to do with my *bruder*."

"That ain't exactly true." When she waited for him to explain, his cheeks turned red. "Ally, it ain't that they blame Carl for the fire or even that they blame May . . . it's just that he's been through so much, and now he's not even Amish. I think they're hoping that if we all pretend they don't have a bond or a connection, then it won't happen. You can't go back in time to change bad things, right? Sometimes, it's best to simply move forward."

The explanation left a lot to be desired, but she didn't exactly disagree. She, Kevin, and her parents had talked a lot about both the fire and Carl's state of mind. They all were worried sick about him. When he was young, he'd been confident and optimistic about pretty much everything. His confidence didn't come from pride; it was just the way he'd

looked at the world. He'd been sure that the Lord didn't create obstacles for his flock to overcome but opportunities to
make his people stronger.

His happy outlook on life used to be mighty annoying.
Now, though, he was so standoffish and closed—well,
they'd all be secretly happy if he showed even a hint of his
former attitude.

None of them thought he was weak or couldn't take care
of himself. But it was also the truth that, more than anything, they'd all just like to push the whole incident from
their minds.

Pretend it had never happened.

Except for the fact that Carl was always going to have
scars, and he'd always have to go to burn units and plastic
surgeons because burned skin didn't age like normal skin.

And he'd never want to be Amish again because he'd become so dependent on technology during his teens.

All that was his business. The problem was that in the
middle of it all, Ally and Walker had fallen in love. Their relationship was a secret that neither wanted to make public
because it was just going to put a whole lot of other people
in awkward positions.

Feeling deflated, Ally nodded. "I wish we didn't have to
sneak around so much."

"Me, too. But Kevin knows about us, right?"

She shrugged. "I think he might. I don't talk about it, and
he doesn't ask." Gazing into his eyes, she added, "I know he
doesn't realize just how serious we are." And they were serious. Really serious.

"I don't think he would be opposed to our marriage."

"I don't think he would either, but I also don't think he
would be in favor of it. It has nothing to do with you; it's
just that there's too much separating us." She sighed. "I feel
like we're Apple Creek's very own Romeo and Juliet."

"I certainly hope not."

"Walker, Romeo and Juliet were in love."

"Maybe so, but they also died, Ally."

She covered her face. "You know I wasn't thinking about that part."

"Of course not." Walker took her hand and covered it with both of his. "I don't know why love has to be so hard."

"I don't either, but everyone says it's never been easy. Every couple goes through difficult times."

"We should give ourselves a deadline."

"Come again?"

"By June first, let's try to get everyone on the same page. That way we can begin planning a wedding."

"Ah, Walker, *nee*, it's not as easy as that."

"Why not?"

Walker was a lot of things. A romantic, he was not. "Because you have to ask me first."

He smiled. "You're serious, aren't you?"

"I'm more than serious, Walker." She was, too. As much as she loved him, she also missed all the normal things other courting couples did. She wanted him to pick her up in his courting buggy. She wanted everyone to look at the two of them and think they were perfect for each other.

In short, she wanted memories to treasure when she was old and stories to share when their children were little.

"Please don't think I'm being silly to yearn to be silly in love."

"Oh, Ally." He pulled her into his arms and kissed her lightly on the lips. After brushing his lips across her cheek, he murmured into her ear, "I would ask you now if I thought it was fair to you."

"So, you do understand?"

Pulling away, he gazed into her eyes. "Of course I do. Believe me, I want you to be my happily engaged fiancée. I want every other man in Apple Creek to know you are mine. One day, I want to see you standing across from me on our wedding day and think about how happy you look. You deserve both of those things."

"I think we both deserve those things, Walker."

The longing in her voice—so full of hope and yearning—made his breath catch. When he spoke, he knew his voice was hoarse, but he didn't care. "Ally, darling, I don't want anything—not even feuding families—to take the future we deserve away from us."

"I don't either."

"I know it will be hard, but when the time is right, I think we're going to need to reveal our secret and make everyone listen."

She swallowed. "Walker, that's going to be a lot."

"I know it will be hard, but you feel the same way, don't you?"

She nodded, though she wasn't sure if she felt completely the same way as Walker. There was a selfish part of her that wanted to shout at May and Carl and their parents and maybe even the whole Amish community that her and Walker's feelings counted, too. They had a right to be happy. She had a right to choose the man she wanted to marry.

She'd even told the Lord that it might be wrong, but she didn't think that He had put only May and Carl next to each on purpose.

He'd placed her and Walker next to each other, too.

But maybe she was wrong in her thinking.

So far, He hadn't answered her prayers.

Not a one.

Chapter 4

Confused by Carl's return—and the fact that he and his family still seemed to resent her, May had found comfort the only way she knew how—by being outside with her beloved herd. About a year after the fire, her father had come home with a fawn-colored female alpaca. He'd been at an auction, had started talking with folks about their alpacas, and somehow ended up bringing one home.

Cupid was sweet but shy. Soon, they discovered that she was also depressed. Alpacas liked to have friends, two others at the very least.

Since her whole family had already fallen in love with Cupid, her father and Walker had gone out and bought two more alpacas—a boy and a girl. Sticking with the Santa's reindeer theme, they'd named them Dancer and Prancer.

Of course, they'd soon learned that alpacas have to be separated by sex—and that each group needs at least three. Off her father had gone again, much to their mother's amusement.

Now, almost five years later, the Schott family had a small

herd of eight alpacas, each named after one of Santa's reindeer. Walker had soon decided that he'd rather farm than
tend to the herd. She'd been so lonely with Carl gone, she'd
taken charge of the herd. That shift had seemed to suit her
father, brother, and the alpacas just fine.

They were silly creatures, shy with strangers, tempera-
mental, skittish, and curious. They also had distinct per-
sonalities, and didn't have a lot of patience for pity parties.

For sure and for certain, her alpacas believed that they
should be the focus of all her attention all the time. Whenever she dared to focus on other things in their presence,
they made their displeasure known. Once Blitzen had even
spit at her.

After helping her mother hang up some laundry and wash
some dishes, May began to feel that same ball of worry she
always felt whenever she thought of Carl. That discomfort
was heightened by her mother's comments and questions.
She was giving May a little bit of space, but it was obvious
that she wanted some answers.

That was why May escaped out the back door toward
the barn. The alpacas might not give her much sympathy,
but at least they wouldn't attempt to give her advice or crit-
icism.

As far as she was concerned, that was a plus.

Glad to focus on her chores and not think about anything
else, May was beaming . . . until she ran into her father, who
was coming out of the barn just as she was heading in. She
barely skidded to a stop.

He curved his hands around her shoulders. "Whoa, dear.
You need to watch where you are going."

"I'm sorry."

He looked at her more closely. "Do you need something, May?"

"*Nee*. My head was in the clouds, that's all. I'm going to go work with the alpacas."

He frowned. "I didn't know that was in your plans. What are you going to work on today?"

Since she hadn't planned to do anything but fuss over Cupid, she blurted the first idea that came to mind. "I'm going to take them to the training pen to work on ringing a bell."

"Alpacas don't need to be performing no tricks, May. They're not pets."

"I haven't forgotten that. But no matter what you say, they enjoy the challenge of learning new things, especially Blitzen. He's so smart. I think sometimes Donner and Prancer annoy him."

"Donner would annoy anyone." Donner was the selfish member of the herd.

"I think he's getting better."

"I hope you're right. Well, good luck with their training, then. Don't stay out here too late."

"I won't." After double-checking that she had a good supply of finely chopped carrots in the pocket of her apron, May walked out to the training pen. She scanned the area, making sure there were no stray branches or trash or other unwanted debris, then went into the barn.

The family had one large barn, but it functioned like two separate ones. The male alpacas were on one side and the females on the other. Unlike horses, the alpacas liked to be in stalls with at least two other members of the same sex. The breeders had warned her parents that all alpacas got skittish and frightened when left on their own. Some even got sick.

After doing a cursory check on the females, she entered the males' section and opened the door so they could go out to the pen.

As usual, Blitzen led the group of three. His black-and-white-speckled fur looked as fluffy and cute as ever. He seemed eager to work with May. His alert, dark eyes seemed to take in everything around him. After the three made an exploratory walk around the pen, they gathered back at her side.

As always, she talked to the animals as if they were her friends—or, rather, her schoolchildren.

"Today we're going to work on bell ringing." Getting out her clicker, she tapped the bell. "Blitz, you go first. Come, please."

Blitzen, pleased to show off and get treats, marched right over to her side. May pressed her clicker and gave him a piece of carrot. "Ring the bell, Blitzen. Could you ring the bell, please?"

Blitzen lifted up his nose and moved the bell. When it rang, she beamed. "Good job, Blitzen. *Gut boo.*" She clicked and gave him another tiny piece of carrot.

Donner stepped forward. He was so curious. He nudged her with his nose.

"You are a *good'un*, Donner. Come to the bell." She moved closer to it and motioned him forward. Donner stepped cautiously but walked to where Blitzen had been standing. After she clicked and gave him a piece of carrot, she said, "Ring the bell."

Donner continued to eye the bell warily, as if he feared that it would reach out and bite him. After five minutes and a lot more coaxing, he finally nudged it with his nose.

"Good job, Donner! Good boy!" She clicked and gave him a piece of carrot. He ate the carrot but didn't act too enthusiastic about either the activity or the treat.

After practicing two more times, he lost interest and went to nibble on some fresh green grass beside Blitzen.

That left just Comet.

Walking up to him, she petted his side gently. He tensed

but allowed her touch. Then, after coaxing him toward the bell, she said, "Ring the bell."

Comet eyed the bell as if it offended him. He didn't move an inch. Instead, he lifted his chin as if he preferred to show off the white lightning-bolt streak on his forehead.

May knew all about his attitude, though. Ignoring his look of disdain, she clicked and tapped the bell. "Come on, Comet. Ring the bell. Please?"

After giving her another disdainful look, the brown alpaca turned and walked away.

"Fine," she said. "But don't blame me when you wish you'd gotten some carrots," she told him. "I know that you don't like to perform tricks, but it's good for your tiny brain, don'tcha think?"

Again, Comet sniffed, as if even the thought of ringing a bell for a carrot was offensive.

"It's good everyone likes your wool, Comet. Otherwise, I don't know what we'd do with you." That was a lie, of course. They'd keep all their alpacas even if they simply stood around just looking cute.

For their part, the alpacas might cry and carry on while they were being sheared, but they danced and leapt around the pens after it was over. The wool was thick and heavy and made them feel overheated.

After going into the barn, she got a cloth and a pick and went back out to attend to Blitzen's hooves, then continued with the next two animals.

Next, she guided them back into the barn and did much the same things with the girls.

Two hours later, after cleaning the stalls, checking the water, and even neatly rearranging the bins for their food and supplements, she was feeling almost like herself.

All she had to do was remind herself that having Carl live next door to her family again might be difficult . . . but it wasn't an insurmountable problem. No matter how hard it was going to be to be ignored by him, she could take it.

Especially since he would soon leave Apple Creek again.

And everything between them—their childhood friendship, their teenage infatuation, their kiss . . . the fire, the hospital stays . . . the pain . . .

Well, it would likely one day become a blur.

Chapter 5

Carl was learning that although one could go home again physically, returning to one's parents' house after a lengthy absence didn't mean that it would feel the same way as before.

Actually, his long-delayed return was turning out to be far different from what he had imagined. It was a little embarrassing to realize that he'd somehow come up with a twisted view of what the other four members in his family would think of him. "I was afraid of this."

Carl had decided when he was driving his truck to Apple Creek that he would do his best to honor his parents' way of living when he was home. Sure, his vehicle was parked in the driveway, and it was unabashedly fancy, too. It was black and had a leather interior and a sunroof. Honestly, it rather gleamed in the sun.

Besides his Chevy Silverado, he'd brought along his cell phone and laptop. They'd become necessary extensions of his life, especially given that he was a project manager with a manufacturing company. He worked at home but was constantly online reviewing plans, organizing data, and developing timelines.

Though he was technically on vacation, he'd assured everyone at Convergent that he would check his email several times a day. He was determined to do that, too . . . though it usually meant that he had to travel to a coffee shop in Medina or Millersburg for an hour at a time. There were neither Wi-Fi nor electrical outlets on the farm.

He'd thought his family would appreciate his efforts to live plain and simple, at least while he was with them.

They hadn't.

But while he'd feared they'd get mad and chastise him for bringing the outside world into their home, the opposite had happened. Kevin, Ally, and his parents were all intrigued. They asked lots of questions about his job, his schedules, and what he liked and didn't like about them.

Instead of resenting that he was different, they seemed to enjoy his differences.

Actually, all of them had thought it was rather funny that he was acting as if fitting in was going to be impossible. It wasn't.

Moreover, all of them were interested in his phone and laptop, his job and his social media accounts. They also enjoyed zipping around Apple Creek in his truck.

"I might still be plain, but I'm not an old man," his father grumbled.

Carl had been so surprised by the statement, all he'd done was nod.

He supposed their willingness to accept the invasion of so many English things into their life was a lesson to him. He'd imagined that the fire and the resulting surgeries had changed only him, but he couldn't have been more wrong. It had changed all of their lives.

However, as much as the acceptance had been a nice surprise, there were other things about coming home that had been very hard to get used to.

His family was constantly hovering. He'd become accustomed to not only living alone, but also only worrying about himself and his own needs. Now, he was back in his small bedroom, sleeping on his twin bed, which was as hard as he remembered, and sharing one bathroom with three other people.

In addition, they seemed to have no compunction about asking him questions and staring at his scars. It rattled him.

And he was currently feeling very rattled.

"No, Ally, I am not going to take off my shirt for you."

"It's not just for me. Mamm wants to see your scars, too."

He dared to glance over at their mother. "Why?"

"No specific reason, Carl . . . I'm just wondering how they look. I haven't seen your left side in years now. Have the scars faded at all?"

Putting down his coffee cup, he folded his arms across his chest. He hoped the gesture demonstrated that he was a grown man rather than giving away what he was really doing, shielding himself.

"I'm not comfortable with everyone seeing my, um, torso."

"I'm sure you aren't."

"So you understand why I don't feel like doing some kind of show-and-tell right now?"

"No . . . because we're not everyone, Carl. We're your family."

"But still. And, um, we're standing here in the living room, Mamm."

"What's wrong with that?"

Of course, the back door opened, and in came both Kevin and Daed. Great.

Kevin leaped right into the conversation like an invited guest. "What's wrong with what?"

"Carl's being shy."

"About what?" Daed asked.

"His body," Ally added. "All I asked was if he'd take off his shirt for Mamm and me, but he's acting like he's going to uncover his private parts."

Wasn't his bare chest allowed to be private? "I'm not acting like that," he protested. "You just took me off guard."

"You know what? I think Carl has every right to want to keep his shirt on," Daed said. Folding his arms over his chest, he continued. "If he doesn't want us to admire the healing that the Lord and the doctors have provided him, I suppose that's his choice."

Whether his father's words were meant to embarrass him or not, he didn't know. But he realized that he might as well get it over with. "You know what? Fine."

He grabbed the bottom of his T-shirt and pulled it up over his head. And then stood there while the four people he loved most in the world stared at his broken, red, uneven, deformed skin. He braced himself, silently waiting for murmurs of dismay followed by expressions of pity.

"Turn around, Carl," his father said.

Shocked by the command, he turned. Now his back was facing them. He could feel the tension flowing from him in waves. One second passed. Then another.

And still no exclamations.

"Well?" he finally asked.

"Well, now, I think you're looking a lot better than I ever guessed you would," Daed said. "Those doctors have done a good job on ya, son."

He jumped when his mother touched his side. "Mamm, what are you doing?"

"Nothing. I just wanted to feel this scar." Her hand lifted. "Does touching it hurt?" she asked in a gentle tone.

He might be uncomfortable, but he couldn't lie. "*Nee.*"

"*Gut*. Look at this ridge, Kevin," Mamm said as she carefully ran a hand along the worst scar on his side. "Why, it's almost smooth."

"*Jah*. It is better," his fourteen-year-old brother announced, as if he was entitled to have an opinion.

Their mother continued. "Oh, Carl. Everything looks so good."

Good? "Mamm—"

"Hush now, son. "Able, look at this one."

When she touched one of the scars where the nerve endings were still giving him grief, he pulled away. "Don't."

"Don't what?"

Irritated, he turned to face her. His mother's hand was up in the air.

"You know. Touch me. Examine my back." Feeling too exposed, he reached for his shirt and pulled it on over his head. When his head popped out, all three members of his family were staring at him in surprise. "What?"

"You know what," Ally said. "Are you really that self-conscious about your body?"

"I would ask if you've seen it, but you just got a good long look. So I think the answer's obvious."

"Does your skin hurt still?" Mamm asked.

"Not really." Well, it did in certain spots, but the doctors said that might always be the case. That knowledge was too disturbing to share.

"Are you not used to anyone seeing or touching the scars?"

His sister's question had multiple connotations. To his mind, she was asking if he'd ever allowed a woman to run her hands over his back. He blushed like a schoolboy. "I don't want to discuss my body anymore. Like, never again."

"I see."

Kevin threw up his hands. "Sorry, Carl. It never occurred to me that you would be so self-conscious."

"If you looked like me, you'd be self-conscious too. You'd wish you were normal."

"Enough of that," Daed said. "You are normal."

"Daed, *danke*, but we know that's a lie. I look . . ." He couldn't say the words out loud.

"You look like you risked your life to save May Schott," he bit out. "That's how you look, son. You look like a hero."

Ally walked to his side and wrapped her arms around his shoulders. "Every time I see those scars, I see a man who risked everything to save someone else. Who went through terrible pain for years. You don't have a single thing to be embarrassed about."

His eyes stung. "I don't know what to say."

"At the very least, praise God and lift your chin, son. There's a reason He put you through so much. And if you ever wondered why you survived, it's because He knew you could handle it." His mother sighed. "I don't know what kind of life you've been living up there in Cleveland, but it's obvious that you should've come home far more often. You need us. Just like we need you."

Chapter 6

"I can't believe the teacher gave us a gift card to Bruno's," May told Walker as they sat down at a table near the front of the Italian restaurant.

"I can't believe that our parents insisted we use it tonight. I was sure Daed would place it in a drawer for a rainy day."

May chuckled. Saving things for another, more catastrophic day was typical of her father. He was a saver and insisted on never using something if it could be enjoyed at a later date. It had been so aggravating when they were younger. "I can only think that they had a good reason. I wonder why they wanted us out of the *haus*?"

"I have no idea." He grinned. "I'm going to choose to believe that Daed noticed how patient you were with the schoolchildren and how gentlemanly I was with their teacher."

She scoffed. "That ain't likely, but I'm not going to question it further. I'm just glad you didn't want to wait a spell."

"There weren't no way I was going to do that. Our father could change his mind tomorrow."

"It's likely he would." She smiled at him as she scanned the menu. "Do you know what you're going to get?"

"I'm leaning toward manicotti."

"Really? I didn't know you liked that."

"I'm not sure if I do or I don't, but I figure it's time to see. What about you?"

"Lasagna."

Her brother rolled his eyes. "You always get lasagna."

"I also always like it. I don't like being surprised, you know."

"Sometimes you need to take a chance. You won't know if you like something or not if you don't give it a try."

"I suppose." Privately, though, she kept thinking about the many meals they'd shared when Walker had been less enthusiastic about his dinner. Since dinners out were such a rarity, she always thought it was a shame that he didn't enjoy his meal more.

"What will you two have?" the server asked.

After they gave her their orders, May relaxed. The good thing about dining with Walker was that it didn't require a lot of conversation. He was just as happy as she to sit quietly and simply enjoy the meal.

He'd just taken a sip of his soda when he stiffened. His expression turned wary. "Prepare yourself, May."

"Why?"

"Because you're in for a doozy of a surprise."

"What are you talking about?" She turned to see what Walker was staring at. Then wished she hadn't.

There, standing right in front of them, was Carl Hilty. He wasn't wearing a hat and had on a long-sleeved, white, oxford-cloth shirt and jeans. The shirt looked pressed—there were creases in the sleeves. He was wearing jeans and tennis shoes, too—and carrying a black canvas satchel. The clothes made him look so English.

When their eyes met, she turned back around. Just as she'd done a time or two when she was twelve and attending the Amish school. She felt like slapping a hand against her forehead. What must he be thinking? This was now the second time that she'd gaped at him as if he was an alien from another planet or something. No doubt Carl thought she was either very rude or very childish.

It was a blessing that Walker had no trouble finding his voice. "Hiya, Carl. Guess you came in for some Italian food, too?"

"I did." He darted a look her way.

"Hi," she squeaked.

Looking rather amused, he nodded. "Hi, May."

Determined to behave like a normal woman instead of a deer in the headlights, she said, "Would you like to join us? It's just my brother and I."

"Thanks, but I'm going to sit at one of the back tables. It's hard to get any kind of Internet at my parents' house, so I go to different places to get online."

"I hadn't thought about that. I bet it's hard for you to get your work done."

"I'm managing."

She drew back. Had he thought she was criticizing him for some reason?

Walker cleared his throat. "How are you finding Apple Creek?"

Humor lit Carl's eyes. "It's exactly like I remembered it. For some reason, I had imagined that the town had grown by leaps and bounds, but that's not exactly the case."

"Ally does like to exaggerate the importance of things around town," Walker said. "The way she describes our community auction makes one think that it rivals Shipshewana's flea market."

Carl nodded. "She's always been like that. She lives her life in superlatives."

"What's that?" May asked.

"Oh, you know. Something isn't good, it's fantastic. Or it's not difficult, it's exhausting."

"Ah."

A line formed between Carl's brows. "Walker, I might be mistaken, but I didn't think our families communicated all that much. How do you know about Ally?"

Her brother's cheeks flushed. "Oh, you know . . . she's always been like that. I assume that she's the same."

"Ah," said Carl. He looked skeptical.

May tried to think of something to ease the tension-filled moment, but she couldn't think of a single thing that would do the trick.

"Here are your orders," the server announced as she approached. "Sir, would you like me to bring you a menu?"

Carl shook his head. "Thanks, but I'm sitting near the back. I . . . I was just saying hello to these folks. Enjoy your meal," he murmured.

"*Danke.* You, too."

His eyebrows rose, but he didn't say another word as he wandered to the back of the restaurant. Unable to stop herself, May watched until he was out of sight. He looked so good and so confident. All those warm feelings she'd harbored for him bubbled to the surface again.

"Do you need anything else?"

May blinked, realizing that the server was still standing by their table—and that she'd noticed the way May had stared after Carl like a lovelorn wallflower. "I don't," she said at last.

"We're fine," Walker added. "Our meals look good."

"It's sure a shame about that man," she said with a soft expression. "I bet he was once really handsome."

Unable to help herself, May lifted her chin. "He still is."

Instantly, the server blushed. "Of course he is. I'm sorry for saying anything."

Walker sipped his water, obviously so he wouldn't start laughing. "Oh, May. Something has got to happen between the two of you. The tension is as thick as . . ."

"Your manicotti sauce?"

Frowning at his plate, he nodded. "I'm wondering if I made a mistake."

Thinking about all the tiny conversational mistakes she'd just made with Carl, and the proprietary way she'd just acted with the server, May nodded. "I know the feeling all too well."

Chapter 7

The evening was so balmy, Walker and Ally had elected to meet on the creek bed. There was a certain bend in the creek that had a wide, flat bank with lots of logs and rocks. It gave them a nice place to sit and watch the stars—and was still private.

Though he was always eager to see Ally, this evening he'd been especially eager. He had news to share about their siblings, and he couldn't wait to hear Ally's thoughts about it.

As he'd hoped, Ally had listened intently the whole time he'd described the visit to Bruno's—and Carl's unexpected appearance there. Unable to help himself, Walker had shared his thoughts about the long looks between May and Carl, and even the way May had been so quick to defend Carl's appearance to the young woman who was their server.

Ally had listened intently, barely asking him a single question until he was finished.

"So that is how everything went today at Bruno's," Walker said when he finished. "There's no doubt about it— something is still going on between the two of them."

"It sure sounds like it. Are you sure Carl kept looking at May?"

"I'm sure. He was obviously trying to be sneaky about it, but he didn't fool me. Carl doesn't hate May, Ally. Honestly, I think he still likes my sister an awful lot."

As he'd hoped, Ally treated the news with enthusiasm. "Wouldn't that be something if Carl and May got together, too?" Ally clasped her hands together. "Our parents could have double weddings—we'd all be related."

As cute as Ally sounded, so full of plans and optimism, Walker wasn't as hopeful. "It would be something—if they'd ever let us all get married . . . and if they'd ever let Carl be a part of an Amish wedding since he's English now."

She sighed. "So it's just a flight of fancy, isn't it? You don't think it's ever going to happen."

Walker hated to spoil her dreams, but he was enough of a realist to come to terms with the fact that not everyone got what they wanted. Wishing for castles and fairy-tale lives led to disappointment. "I'm not saying that I don't believe in all of us getting together and becoming one big family. It just feels doubtful."

"I guess you're right."

Walker hated to see Ally look so crestfallen. She was such a good person, and she did so much for other people. Why, here she was, sneaking around with him because she didn't want to upset her parents. "I think we've been sneaking around enough, don't you?"

"*Jah*, but I don't see that we have a choice. It isn't like we can run away or do our own things. You help your father and May with both the farm and the alpacas, and I help my mother with the house and garden."

"I understand."

"I can't just leave, Walker. Not only is it different for a

woman, but my *mamm* has arthritis. She physically can't run a house on her own."

"I haven't forgotten." He scooted closer to her and clasped her hand between both of his own. "I'm not trying to upset you . . . but I do think it's time we allowed ourselves to be happy, too. We're both twenty years old. It's past time we stopped sneaking around at night like we were little kids."

"I agree, but what can we do?"

"Let's give ourselves a date to come out in the open. Our parents all love us. They might get mad and make threats, but their disappointment won't last forever."

She blinked. "And then you'll be able to come courting."

"I will. And take you out in the buggy, too."

"Who would've ever imagined that the simple act of riding by your side in a buggy would sound like a fairy tale?"

Walker wrapped an arm around her shoulders. "Me. Letting the whole world know that you're my girl—and one day *mei frau* will be wonderful."

"*Wunderbar.*"

"*Jah.*"

"Maybe if we break the ice, it will help Carl and May overcome their problems, too."

"I hope so." Tired of spending all their time talking about the rift between their families, he pulled her closer. "It's getting late. Can we talk about something else now? Or maybe not even talk at all?"

Leaning closer, she peeked up at him through her eyelashes. "What do you think we could possibly do?"

He didn't reply with words—there was a much better way to respond. Curving his hands around her cheeks, he kissed her lips, enjoying the sweet sensation.

Loving that their kisses were a prelude to what would surely be a lifetime together. One day.

* * *

When Ally crawled in through her bedroom window, she just about had a heart attack to find Carl sitting on the chair next to her desk. When she saw him, she inhaled sharply, then had to bite down on her lip so she wouldn't squeal.

"Carl Hilty, what are you doing in here?"

"Obviously, I was waiting up for you." He scowled. "I've also been trying to convince myself that you were fine and not hurt or abducted or something."

"Oh, calm down. We live in Apple Creek, not the big city. You shouldn't have worried about me. I am just fine."

He turned on the flashlight and looked at her closely. Ally felt as if he was noticing every single wrinkle in her dress, every hair out of place . . . and that she had just-kissed lips. "Turn that light off before you wake up Kevin."

He turned the flashlight off and tossed it on her mattress but remained where he was. "You might as well sit down." His voice turned sarcastic. "I'm guessing that you had a good time tonight?"

Instead of answering—it wasn't any of his business, after all—she asked him a question of her own: "How did you even know I left?"

"First of all, I used to do the same thing."

"You did?"

"Uh, don't you remember a certain barn on the Schotts' property? You didn't think Mamm and Daed let me go visit May at night with their blessing, did ya?" Why hadn't she thought about that?

"I never thought about it."

"Anyway, secondly, I opened your door because you didn't answer my knock and saw your window open."

"So you just decided to camp out until I returned?"

He crossed one leg over the other. "Pretty much."

"Next time, don't."

He frowned. "How often do you go out?"

"That is none of your business." She held her breath, waiting for him to argue or get offended.

But he surprised her. "You're right. It isn't. You're a grown woman, and I've been gone a long time. I have no right to keep tabs on you." He looked at her intently. "I'm still worried about you."

Mentally weighing the pros and cons of confiding in him, Ally realized that she wanted to tell him the truth. No, she needed to tell him. "I was out with Walker Schott."

He got to his feet. "Why?"

She rolled her eyes. Her brother's head could be so thick. "Why do you think, Carl? He and I are secretly dating."

"Really?"

"Of course, really. I wouldn't make that up."

"When did this happen?"

She closed the window behind her and sat down on the edge of her bed. "You might as well have a seat." Carl sat but still looked at her expectantly. "Walker and I got closer after the fire. You were in the hospital, of course. And Mamm and Daed were there with you."

"Where were you and Kevin? Did someone look after you here? I'm embarrassed that I never thought about that."

"From what I heard, you were sedated almost the entire first month you were gone, so there's no reason you should've been thinking about that. To answer your question, Aunt Darla stayed with us."

"But Aunt Darla doesn't even get along with Mamm and Daed."

"I know. But she wanted to help, and our parents were in no position to refuse. So Darla watched me and Kevin, which meant that we got to do practically whatever we wanted." She waved a hand. "Kevin and I were worried about you, and about May, too, so we went to their house a lot. Those first couple of nights, May was in the hospital, too. Both of her parents were there, but then, eventually, only Marjorie stayed and Ben went home because of the alpacas. Then, of course, there was the barn raising and all the work involved with that.

"Eventually, Kevin went over to help Walker and Ben. I went along because it was boring at home with Aunt Darla. Walker and I became closer."

"If you two got close, how did everything fall apart? When did everyone stop speaking?"

Thinking back, Ally shrugged. "I can't tell you an exact moment, Carl. Not really. At first, both Mamm and Daed were with you, and Aunt Darla was attempting to watch over me and Kevin. But after a month, Daed came back. He was different then. He wouldn't hardly talk about you, just said that you were in a lot of pain and that you'd never be the same. He was so bitter.

"Darla only lasted a couple of days with him, then she left, too."

"I can see that happening."

"I don't blame her. She wasn't all that fond of living without electricity. Plus, Daed wasn't all that patient with her cooking efforts." Suddenly remembering all their arguments, she added, "Darla kept telling him that there was nothing wrong with grilled hot dogs and hamburgers, especially since he wouldn't help her with the dishes."

"What about you and Walker . . ."

"Oh. Well, when Daed got back, he was quieter. Really subdued. He said it was hard to watch you in so much pain. He was upset with the Lord."

"It wasn't God's fault."

"Well, he wanted someone to blame. Then, um, when

Preacher Elias told him that it wasn't good to blame the
Lord for lightning bolts, Daed started blaming Marjorie and
Ben. And then, somehow, he decided that May was the real
culprit."

"She didn't start the fire."

"I guess May felt guilty and said that you were hurt because she froze and didn't run out of the barn fast enough."
Feeling guilty for bringing up the fire and all the drama and
hurt feelings once again, Ally finished the story.

"Eventually, Mamm came back, but she cried all the time
because she felt guilty for leaving you in the hospital. Kevin
and I didn't know what to do. That's when Daed started
saying that he didn't want our family to have anything to do
with the Schott family."

"Wow."

Ally nodded. "It's been a mess."

"How close are you and Walker?"

"We're in love."

He looked completely taken aback. "You sound so certain."

"That's because I am." She waved a hand. "When you
know, you know, I think."

"I'm starting to realize that I need to stop thinking of you
as my little sister."

"I hope so. I grew up, Carl." Unable to help herself, she
added, "And, sorry, but I'm pretty sure that I have more of
my life together than you do."

He ran a hand through his dark brown hair. "I reckon you
do. So, um, what are you two going to do? Have you decided?"

"Sometimes I feel like it's all we've been talking about.
Personally, I've been wanting to wait. I mean, we didn't get
super serious until about a year ago."

"And Walker?"

"Walker is tired of sneaking around. He wants to get everything out in the open. As far as he's concerned, it's better for everyone to understand how we really feel, but it's not that easy, Carl." Eyeing her older brother, dressed in his English clothes, with his steady, well-paying job, she felt a twinge of jealousy. Not for his choices or his lifestyle—but because he had already figured out his future.

Well, at least a lot of it.

He was studying her, sympathy in his eyes. "Putting everything out in the open sounds good, but I think it might be really hard. I could be wrong, but I think the consequences are going to be harder for you than for Walker."

"I fear you're right." Lowering her voice, she added, "You know how our Daed is. He's stubborn and is always sure he's right."

Carl nodded. "Always."

"I can't imagine him suddenly being okay with me marrying Walker. If he refuses to see reason, I'm going to have to move out."

Carl kicked his legs out. "Which will be hard not only on you, but on Mamm too."

"Yep. I do a lot around here. Sometimes I'm pretty sure Mamm doesn't even realize I do so many of the chores anymore. She just knows they get done."

"Like the laundry and cooking?"

"Like the mending and selling eggs and sweeping the walkways and cleaning the bathrooms."

"Like everything."

"I hate to sound like Cinderella, but I do sometimes feel a bit overworked and underappreciated." She fell back on her bed. "So, Carl, that's how my life is."

"Everything is a real mess."

Her brother sounded so depressed about it all, she chuckled. "*Jah*. It's a huge mess, actually. The easiest thing for Walker and me would be to break up, but I can't."

"That's not the easiest thing at all. You can't break your heart just because our father wants to blame someone for an accident."

"But what about Mamm?"

"I'm sorry, but Mamm and Daed are going to have to come around and see reason. They can't believe that you don't want to do anything but clean up after everyone and take care of Mamm for the rest of your life."

"I don't mind taking care of her, Carl. I love Mamm. I just want to be happy, too."

"Don't apologize for that. We all want to be happy."

Though she still felt a little melancholy, she smiled at him. Carl wasn't able to make everything better, but confiding in him made her insides feel better.

"Thanks for listening to me."

"Ally, I might not have been here all along, but you know I care about you. That never stopped."

"Will you do me a favor?"

"I'll try."

"Will you please not stay away so long ever again? The phone calls weren't enough, Carl."

Pain filled his eyes, but he nodded. "You're right. They weren't enough. Not by a long shot." He waved a hand. "Al, I feel like I'm at least partly to blame for this situation."

"For what? Me sneaking out to see Walker?"

Still looking troubled, he nodded. "*Jah*."

"Walker and I are adults. We know what we want. But . . . I wouldn't mind a little support from you."

His expression softened. Standing up, he bent down and kissed her brow. "You've got it. And I won't stay away for so long ever again. I promise."

She was afraid to hope. "Do you mean it?"

He nodded. "With everything I am."

"All right then." Some of the pressure inside of her eased. At long last.

After Carl went back to his own room, Ally rolled onto her side. For once, instead of worrying about the future, she gave thanks for her blessings.

It was a nice change.

Chapter 8

It was planting season. Crouching in the middle of her family's large garden, May tried to feel some of her mother's enthusiasm, but she'd really rather be working with the alpacas, as Walker was.

Her mother would have none of it, though. As far as she was concerned, every woman needed to know how to plant a garden and harvest its bounty. It didn't matter if one was a much better seamstress, house cleaner, chef, or alpaca breeder. If one ate, one had to garden.

May reckoned her mother had a point, so she didn't put up a fight. But, as much as she enjoyed the fruits of their labor the rest of the year, digging holes in the dirt was not her favorite task.

"*Ack*, May!" her mother called out. "What's keeping ya? You should have planted that whole row of potatoes and carrots by now."

"I'm working on it."

Getting to her feet, her mother stretched. "I suggest you work on it a little bit harder. Otherwise, you'll still be there come nightfall, ain't so?"

Her mother did love to exaggerate. "I'll get it done. Before it gets dark, too."

"*Gut.* I'm going to get cleaned up and go visit Frannie Abrams. She didn't come to the *kaffi* Mary Walker hosted yesterday. I heard she was under the weather."

"I'm sure she'll be glad of your company."

"I expect so." Walking closer, she frowned. "Those holes look a bit shallow, dear. Any job is worth doing well, ain't so?"

"*Jah*, Mamm." When her mother continued to stand there expectantly, May said the words she was obviously waiting to hear. "I'll make sure the holes aren't too shallow."

"*Gut.*"

May picked up the spade and dug another three holes, each one a good inch deeper than the ones she'd dug earlier. Then she dutifully planted the potato seedlings and neatly covered each with dirt.

An earthworm appeared, and May assumed it was as annoyed as she felt. "Don't blame me, worm. I don't want to be here either."

She continued on, digging, planting, and covering as her mother carried out a basket of food for Frannie and loaded it into the buggy.

May turned the corner and began checking the next row for stray rocks as her mother hitched their mare Debbie up to the buggy and finally clip-clopped down the drive.

Only when her mother was well out of sight did she stop.

Standing up again, she stretched her arms above her head and contemplated the long row that needed to be planted. It looked never-ending.

May sighed. Since Walker was in the fields with Daed and the alpacas, she was essentially alone.

Deciding it was time for some water, she walked to the house, put ice in a mason jar, then filled it from the tap. She sat down on the front porch and wondered what she'd rather be doing instead of planting root vegetables.

"Anything," she muttered out loud.

Guilt and embarrassment coursed through her at thinking such selfish thoughts. She had no reason to be unhappy or to feel dissatisfied. She had a loving family and a bright mind. She had good friends like Camille.

She'd survived the fire.

That was what her life always came down to, she realized. She'd survived, so she should be happy and grateful. She shouldn't want anything more.

Well, anything beyond Carl's forgiveness.

As if she'd conjured him up, a figure approached. She wouldn't have known who he was—except for that ball cap.

Apprehension, followed by excitement, filled her as she hurried down the steps to meet him. Only when she was halfway down did she remember just how much she resembled a ragamuffin. She was in an old, faded-green dress, wore dirty boots, and a straw hat covered her *kapp*.

It was tempting to run inside and change, but he'd already seen her. Besides, it was wrong to be so prideful.

No, it was foolish to even imagine that he would care what she looked like. He didn't like her anymore.

Slowing her footsteps, she continued to stare at him. How could a man she hadn't seen in six years still look so familiar?

When they were within speaking distance, she summoned her courage. "Hiya, Carl."

"*Gut matin*, May."

A shiver ran through her. His voice was deeper, scratchier-sounding than she remembered. She wondered if it was simply how his voice was, or if he'd incurred some sort of damage to his throat in the fire that she was unaware of. "May I help you with something?"

He stopped. "Ah, not exactly. I came to speak with you." He stuffed his hands in his pockets. "If you have any time to spare?"

"Of course I do. I . . . well, I am supposed to be planting carrots and potatoes, but I'm taking a break."

He turned to the field. Sure enough, there was her basket, the towel for her knees, the little spade she'd been using. "Do you still hate to garden?"

"Hate is kind of a strong word to describe my feelings. But yes." She couldn't deny the truth.

His expression softened. "Come on, then."

Noticing that he'd started toward the field, she rushed to his side. "Carl, what are you doing?"

"Helping you plant."

"*Nee*! You mustn't."

"Why?"

"You know why. You're not a farmer anymore."

"Just because I work on a computer doesn't mean I don't remember how to tend to a garden." When she still looked skeptical, he raised one eyebrow. "May, what's going on? Do you really not think that I can still handle a spade and a couple of potato eyes?"

His tone stung. She wondered why he was taking offense at her words, and she wondered why he'd come over in the first place. "I'm sure you can handle whatever you want. What I meant is that it's not right to make a guest do my chores."

He looked away for a moment before clearing his throat. "Forgive me. What I meant to say was that I don't mind helping you."

"*Danke*, but if we're going to talk after all this time, I'd rather talk someplace other than in the middle of a garden." Summoning her mother's good manners, she added, "Perhaps you'd like to come in for some lemonade or a cup of coffee?"

"*Danke*, but I'd rather do something while we talk. Time

might have passed since we've had a real conversation, but that doesn't mean we need to be formal."

She still didn't move. "Honestly, Carl."

"Nope. I'm not gonna let you argue. Now, come on, May. Stop stalling and come out to the field. We might as well get this done."

She wasn't sure what was going on, but she decided to stop arguing. Since he was ahead, she quickened her pace. She pretended not to stare at him, but it was almost impossible to do anything but that. He was so tall now. And his hair was so short. She liked the way it was almost entirely hidden under his baseball cap. She liked his T-shirt, too.

And, yes, the way he filled it out.

"Do I look as terrible as you imagined?"

She skidded to a stop. "What?"

"I can feel you staring at me. If you're going to stare at my skin, you might as well be open about it."

"I wasn't staring at your scars, Carl."

"You don't need to lie."

Now she was getting mad. "I really wasn't staring at them. Believe it or not, it's the truth."

"You expect me to believe that?"

"*Nee.* Not if this is how you go about your life. If you want to know the truth, I *was* staring at you. However, I wasn't staring at your scars. I was noticing how you've changed. You're taller. Your hair is short. You grew up." Since he had turned to face her, she propped her hands on her hips. "Do you really find it so hard to believe that I don't notice anything about you beyond those scars?"

"I'm sorry." Obviously frustrated with himself, he sighed. "You're exactly right. Out in the world, I forget about the scars on my face and body. Most people I deal with are so used to them, no one ever mentions them. I guess it feels different here."

"In Apple Creek."

"*Jah*. I . . . I fear I've become so self-conscious that I've forgotten how to behave in public."

"It seems like you've learned to manage just fine in public. Maybe what you've forgotten is how to behave around friends."

He stared at her for a moment before walking forward. "Is that what we are?"

Now what was she supposed to do with that question? "I know what I want us to be," she replied. "I would like us to be friends again."

Carl stopped at her row and knelt down next to her trowel. "Is this where you stopped?"

"*Jah*."

Easily, he dug a hole. "Carrots or potato?"

"Potato."

He tossed in a seedling and covered it up neatly before digging another hole.

Feeling even more confused, she knelt down, took the trowel after he dug a hole, and then dug another. Of course, it took her twice as much time as Carl.

He took it from her. "How about I dig the holes and you plant?"

"All right."

Whether he'd been looking for her approval or was just determined to complete the task, Carl seemed happy to not talk. She supposed that gave her plenty of time to think, but all she seemed to be able to do was wonder "Why?"

Why had Carl come over? Why had he said that he wanted to talk to her but so far hadn't said anything much? Why had he decided to bring her out to the garden to plant vegetables?

And why, after so many years of ignoring her, was he paying her any mind?

Feeling rather annoyed, she tossed another potato eye in the ground and covered it up. Yes, she might have used a little bit more force than was necessary.

Carl, kneeling on the ground, looked up. "Did the dirt offend you?"

"*Nee.*"

"Then?"

"Carl, I'm feeling confused. Why did you come over here?"

He froze, then sat down on the ground. "I wanted to tell you that I didn't recognize you the other day . . . until it was too late."

"Say again?" Of all the things he could've chosen to talk about, that was the last thing she'd expected.

"You heard me."

He was so prickly. "Carl, maybe you thought that I could read your mind six years ago, but I couldn't. I still can't. If you have something to say to me, you're gonna have to say it loud and clear. And speak less cryptically."

He sighed. "All right, fine. *Mei shveshtah*, Ally, thinks that you might be thinking I hate you. I wanted to let you know that I don't."

"You came over, out of the blue, to let me know you don't hate me."

He blinked. "*Jah.* That's what I just said." Then, just as if he'd commented on the fine day they were having, he picked up the trowel and dug another hole.

May tossed in another piece of potato and covered it up. What was she supposed to say to that? That she was glad? That she didn't hate him either?

Just as she felt another wave of frustration take hold of her, the Lord intervened.

Child. Speak from your heart.

"I'm glad you don't hate me. I don't hate you either."

His hands paused. "No?"

She shook her head. "I really don't." Encouraged by the Lord jumping into the conversation, she added, "I'm glad you're back. You've been gone too long."

He blinked again, then got to his feet. "I'm not here to stay, May. I only intend to visit for a little while."

"Oh. I thought . . . Never mind."

He stood up again. "I've dug all the holes for you. That should help, I reckon."

Then, to her amazement, he started walking away.

May jumped to her feet. "Hold on, Carl. That's it? You come over, dig some holes, and leave?"

"I came over to do what I needed to do."

She hurried over to his side. "But what about everything else? What should we do next?"

His expression softened—well, as much as it could, since part of the right side of his face was frozen in place. "There isn't anything to do next, May. It's not like we have a future."

She gaped at him as he strode back across the field and down her driveway. Carl had left her more confused than ever. Yes, he'd just given her a gift, but he'd also left another scar on her heart.

She now had to figure out what to do about that. She had a feeling it wasn't something that a Band-Aid could easily fix.

Chapter 9

"That's a dangerous game you're playing, May," Walker murmured.

With a start, May turned from petting Prancer and Vixen. "Petting alpacas? Not hardly. You know Prancer and Vixen enjoy the company." Looking down at Curly, their Australian shepherd, she smiled fondly. "Curly ain't real good at conversation, you know."

"I'm talking about Carl visiting you. Have you two been seeing each other on the sly?"

"Absolutely not. I haven't talked to him in years."

"So why did he come by?"

"I think he wanted to clear the air between us." After giving Prancer the last bit of his supplement, she turned to face her brother. "Walker, what is wrong? Are you worried that he might hurt me?"

"Not at all. I was worried, however, when you didn't want him around."

"I'm still not sure how I feel about seeing him." She thought for a moment. "I honestly never thought he'd come back here. And he ignored my letters and phone calls."

"His family went to see him in the city a couple of times a year."

"How do you know that?"

"One hears things . . ."

She wondered what he meant but decided not to press him. "Well, anyway, I was just checking on the alpacas. Tomorrow is supposed to be nice, so I'm going to have them out for most of the day."

"*Jah*, that sounds good. I scheduled three tours on Saturday."

She smiled at Vixen, who especially loved tour groups. "You lucky girl, you're going to get to show off your pretty white coat," she teased, gently rubbing the animal's side.

Vixen stood still for a moment, then seemed to have had enough of that and moved away.

"Don't you sometimes wonder how we ended up with eight alpacas?"

"*Nee*, and you shouldn't either. We were both there when Dasher was born, and when Daed rescued Blitzen and Vixen from that awful farm east of here."

"I don't mean literally, I meant that when we were little, I didn't even know what an alpaca was. Now our whole lives seem to revolve around them."

He frowned, and May felt confused. "I'm sorry, but I still don't see what the problem is."

"I just don't know if I want to work with them the rest of my life."

"You don't have to. I do most of the work. It's by choice, too. I'm good at working with the alpacas."

"You are. That's not my problem."

"What is?" When he hesitated again, she said, "Walker, I feel like you're trying to tell me something without actually telling me anything. I can't read your mind."

"I do have something to tell you, but I'm not real sure how to go about it."

"Maybe you should just dive in."

He nodded. "I've been secretly seeing Ally Hilty."

"Say again?"

"It's been going on for a while," her brother added. "Years."

She was completely confused. "Walker, I'm not going to lie. I guessed you liked Ally, but I didn't know that anything had come of it. Why are you only telling me now?"

"Carl found out. He was in her room when she snuck back in the other night."

"Did you not trust me to keep your secret?"

"I don't know." He looked away. "Maybe I felt guilty. Maybe . . . maybe I knew that if I told you, I'd feel like I had to do something about our secret courting." Looking troubled, he added, "Are you upset?"

"Yes, but not because of your relationship. I'm upset about the situation between her family and ours."

His laugh was humorless and tinged with pain. "You can join the club then. Ally and I have been upset about this feud for a long time."

"I'm pretty sure Ally's parents blame me for Carl's burns. And for him staying away. For everything, actually."

"Nothing that happened is your fault, May."

"I've learned that the truth doesn't always count for much—not when hearts are involved."

He studied her for a long moment. "I reckon you're right."

Meeting his gaze, May said, "That doesn't help much, though, does it?"

"*Nee.*"

Chapter 10

Walker was glad he had a plate of roast beef in front of him. Otherwise, the conversation surrounding their evening meal would feel even worse than it already did.

From the moment he and Daed had gotten in from the fields, all conversation had revolved around Carl's visit—and how May had received him, even though they had been alone.

Walker had been mildly amused at his mother's shocked attitude—until he'd realized that she was completely serious. She thought it was scandalous for his twenty-year-old sister and their next-door neighbor to converse without a chaperone.

He had no idea what Mamm was going to say if she ever found out about the way he and Ally had been sneaking around for years . . . but maybe she wouldn't have too much to say about it. Ever since the fire, she seemed to have a laser-like focus on his sister.

To Walker's dismay, Daed was just as concerned about Carl's visit, but not for propriety's sake. No, he was concerned that she'd been speaking to someone from the Hilty family. As far as his father was concerned, life would be better if there was a brick wall dividing their properties.

Or, better yet, if the Hiltys moved away. Far, far away.

As dinner continued without any end in sight, Walker decided that he, too, wished he was anyplace else.

"What do you think, Walker?"

He set his fork down. "About what, Mamm?"

She raised her eyebrows. "Haven't you been listening? What do you think May should do next?"

"Well, it ain't my call, is it?"

"*Danke*, Walker," May whispered.

Their mother wasn't about to accept his noncommittal response. "You have a right to an opinion. We live next door to Carl Hilty, you know."

"I don't have any problem with any member of the Hilty family. It doesn't sound as if Carl has a problem with May, either. He came over to see her."

"Carl came over to tell May that he doesn't hate her," their mother replied. "He didn't come calling."

May cleared her throat. "Excuse me."

Walker shot her a sympathetic look but still ignored the interruption. "Well, I happen to think that's a good thing, don't you?" he asked. "Or would you rather Carl had come courting?"

"We're being serious, Walker," Daed grumbled.

"I am, too. I think everyone in this house spends far too much time worrying about our next-door neighbors. We should all learn to get along and move on from the fire."

"How can we? The barn was on our property."

"Yes, it was. And folks could also make the argument that Carl's burns are May's fault, but we all know that isn't the truth."

"You don't think so?" May asked. "He was in the barn because of me."

"And for himself. You two were sixteen and seventeen. You were courting. And it was an accident."

"So what do you think May should do?" Mamm asked. Yet again.

Maybe it was the fact that the dinner conversation had gone on too long . . . or that he was sick of always talking about the fire. Or simply because he wanted to start his own life with Ally, but Walker had finally had enough. "I think my sister should move on and think about something else. Think about someone else. Do something with her time. Or, at the very least, realize that there isn't anything in the world she can do to change the past. If she does that, then maybe the rest of us can move on, too."

"Walker, that was a selfish thing to say," May exclaimed.

"I don't think so. I think I'm allowed to speak my mind." Casting an eye at Mamm, who seemed frozen, he added, "I love you, May, but I'm sick and tired of everyone acting as if no one else in this family has any dreams or goals beyond making you happy."

"That's not fair. I haven't done anything to make you feel that way."

"Come, now. You've done everything you could over the years. You pined for Carl, complained about your leg, and even made sure that we all knew you were unhappy here."

"Just because I've been at a loss about what to do with my life, it doesn't mean I expected special attention."

"Are you sure about that?"

May froze.

His father's jaw tightened. "I'd like you to leave this table, Walker. I don't know where this . . . this tirade of yours is coming from."

"That's because I've been holding everyone together. Every morning, I get up, tend to the animals, then go work in the fields."

"I thought you liked farming."

"I do, but I . . ." He had to say it. He finally, finally had to come clean about his secret. "I'm in love with Ally," he blurted.

May froze. Her mother gasped. And her father?

He was staring at Walker as if he'd just started speaking in riddles. "Come again?" Daed said.

On another day, Walker reckoned he'd find his father's astonishment amusing. At the moment, it simply irritated him. "If you want to play this game, then I will, too. I said that I'm in love with Ally, as in Ally Hilty. Carl and Kevin Hilty's sister."

His mother's mouth opened, then closed quickly. "How do you know Ally?"

"Ah, because I've lived next door to her all my life?" he asked sarcastically. When his parents still gaped at him, he rolled his eyes. "Surely you all haven't forgotten that Ally and me were friends back when Carl and May did everything together. We just stayed friends when the rest of you decided to start casting stones."

"But that's impossible," Mamm retorted. "I've never seen you spend time with her."

"That's because we've been forced to sneak around like teenagers."

"Do her parents know about this? Have they been encouraging it?" Mamm looked at Daed. "Ben, I think you should do something."

Daed folded his arms over his chest. "I reckon you might be right."

Walker had had enough. Standing up, he shook his head. "Well, I now have my proof that none of you give much thought to my well-being. Here I finally share a secret that I've been keeping for years. I also admitted that not only have I been seeing Ally, but I am in love with her . . . and all you three seemed concerned about is this ridiculous feud between our families."

"That's not fair."

"You're right. I don't think it's fair at all." He threw his napkin on the table. "Consider this my announcement. I'm going to move out soon and find my own place."

"You can't do that."

"I fear I don't have a choice. May here might be content to be discontented, but I'm tired of waiting for the right time to be happy. Now I'm going to go check on the chickens and those blasted alpacas."

Chapter 11

As much as Carl loved his job at Convergent, now that he was living at home in Apple Creek, there were moments when he felt as if everything that was so crucial at work wasn't all that important in the grand scheme of things.

Unfortunately, his change in attitude wasn't at all helpful when his boss was talking his ear off.

Whit's voice had slowly become more and more clipped over the last five minutes.

"Carl, I know you hear what I'm saying, don't you? We need you to come back to the office." Barely stopping to breathe, he added, "Don't forget, an opportunity like this doesn't come along more than once in a blue moon. It would be a shame not to take advantage of it."

Holding the phone to his ear, Carl stared at his laptop screen and tried to summon some interest in what Whit was saying. So far, he hadn't succeeded.

"Whit, I was honest with you when we met in your office. I told you that I felt I continue to do a good job working remotely. You agreed it wouldn't be a problem."

"I know that's what I said, but this deal with Crocker Tires hadn't come up."

"I realize that, and I want to work with you on it. But I just got back to my family. They won't understand if I leave right away, and frankly, I'm not sure I want to do that to them."

"Can we compromise? Maybe you could come in on Mondays?"

"Let me think about that."

"What in the world do you need to think about?"

Carl clenched his fist. He hated when Whit pushed and pushed, ignoring any explanations that he gave. He supposed Whit had to do it. Everyone knew their team leader felt a lot of pressure from upper management.

However, Carl had begun to learn that always giving the answer his manager wanted to hear wasn't necessarily the best option.

"I'd like to have a real plan in place before I promise to help you out."

A second passed before Whit exhaled. "I understand. Let me know in a couple of days."

"Thank you. In the meantime, I've got to jump on a call and help Wendy on her project."

"Good enough. Thanks, Carl."

Carl put his phone back on the wooden table in the back of the Coffee Connection. It was what his mother would call a "mighty cute *kaffi* shop," though he only thought about it in terms of having the best Internet reception in Apple Creek. He typed some notes, clicked on another screen, and wrote two emails, then checked the time. He'd been there three hours. After his next call, he could probably leave.

He just wasn't sure where to go.

When he'd initially made plans to come back to Apple Creek, a big part of his motivation was to help out his parents on the farm. Now that he was there, he realized his family had moved on just fine without him. His parents weren't struggling at all. Kevin and Ally not only helped with the farming but seemed content to eventually either move to the *dawdi haus,* their grandparents' former home, or a place nearby. His siblings would continue to care for the farm.

They had all missed him, especially Ally, but it was achingly apparent that his grand plan of swooping in and being a huge help to one and all was unnecessary.

When his phone rang again, it was Wendy. "Hey, can we Zoom instead of just talk? I want to show you some graphics I've been working on."

"All right. I'm in a coffee shop, though . . ."

"That's fine. My office is a section of our laundry room. I'll send you the link now."

Standing up, he ordered another cup of coffee. When he sat back down, the link was available. Five minutes later, he was staring at Wendy, and she seemed to be looking at him just as closely.

He knew Wendy was single and about his age. She also had long blond hair and hazel eyes. He supposed she was pretty, but he never thought about her appearance too much—it was her personality that made her attractive.

He realized then that, though they'd met in person once before, he'd been in long sleeves. Now, here he was with a baseball cap on and his scarred left arm in full view.

If she was taken aback by his mottled skin, she did a good job of covering it up. "Carl, look at you in short sleeves. It must be warm there."

"It's seventy degrees."

"It sounds like heaven." She grimaced. "It's sleeting here."

"Ah, yes. I forgot you're up in Minnesota. Well, show me what you've got."

In her typical Wendy way, she started talking fast and

holding up diagrams in her hands. She also clicked a couple of buttons to show a map of what she was describing.

He was so focused, he wasn't aware of too much going on around him—well, nothing beyond the café door opening and closing and a few people standing in line.

At the end of the call, Wendy said, "What do you think? Have I bitten off more than I can chew?"

"Maybe."

She laughed. "That's why I told Whit I love working with you, Carl. You never fail to tell it to me like it is."

Happy that she wasn't arguing with him—and that they'd gotten so much done, he'd leaned back in his chair and picked up his coffee. "For better or worse, right?"

"Absolutely. So, how are you liking being back home?"

"I like it. It's going to take a bit of adjusting, though."

"I imagine it is." Her voice slowed.

Realizing his coworker was looking at something behind him, he turned—and realized that May was standing just over his shoulder and was looking at both him and the screen intently. When she noticed he'd turned, her face turned bright red before she darted back out the door.

Looking back at the screen, he said, "Sorry, Wendy, but I need to go."

"Do you know that Amish girl? She seemed really upset."

"I do know her, and I'm afraid you're right."

"Sorry. Since we usually just talk about work, I forget you grew up Amish."

"There's nothing to apologize for. I forget you have two toddlers at home most of the time. But I do need to go."

Her expression turned concerned. "I hope everything's okay."

"I'm sure it will be. I . . . well, I think it would be a good idea if I go talk to her. I'll work on everything you proposed and let you know what we can do."

"When do you think you might get back to me?"

"Three days?"

She didn't look happy, but she nodded. "All right. Thanks. Bye now."

As soon as they disconnected, he unplugged his computer and gathered his things together as quickly as possible. Then he went out the door. He didn't know if there was a chance of finding May, but he was sure going to try.

He'd recognized that look in her eyes. It was hurt. He might not be close to her anymore, but he knew that expression.

There were some things one never forgot.

Chapter 12

May was mortified. The woman Carl had been talking to on his computer had seen her jealous expression. Had she told him?

Did Carl know that she was jealous of the attractive blonde on his computer screen? If so, he was the type to bring it up.

All she wanted to do was disappear. Since that wasn't possible, May elected to walk as fast as she could through town. If the Lord was feeling benevolent, maybe she'd even get to her favorite park before anyone noticed what a wreck she was.

She truly was a wreck, which was a real shame because there was no reason for her to be. Any "special" relationship that she and Carl had enjoyed was long gone by now. She could pretend that there was still a bond between them, but she knew that would be a lie. The fact of the matter was that six years ago she'd caused his life to change.

For the worse.

One couldn't pretend that they were the same people.

Why, she wasn't even the same person, and she barely had any scarring. She'd only spent a few days in the hospital after the fire.

Head down, she walked past the Dollar Store, a gas station, and the new sandwich shop. She pretended she didn't see the bishop chatting with Mary Walker and prayed neither of them noticed her.

Quickening her pace, she reached the park, turned right on the first path, and finally . . . finally reached the creek. After scanning the area, she breathed a sigh of relief and sat down on the iron bench. A widow had placed it there a few years ago after her husband had passed on to Heaven. There was a tiny brass plaque on it with an inscribed verse from Hebrews inscribed: "Instead, they were longing for a better country—a heavenly one."

The bench had caused a minor uproar when it showed up. Some folks felt it interfered with the natural beauty of the area. Apple Creek's mayor hadn't paid them any mind, however. May was glad about that. She not only liked having a place to sit where her dress wouldn't get dirty, but she also loved the sentiment. As far as she was concerned, more people should enjoy each moment and give thanks.

"Which you seem to have forgotten to do," she muttered to herself. "You're being selfish and more than a little foolish, too." She couldn't deny that.

Had she really thought Carl was going to live with the English, work a job in the outside world, and never date?

Worse, had she actually imagined that a pretty woman wouldn't find him to be attractive?

No. That hadn't surprised her. What had surprised her was her jealousy. She was jealous of a woman who had every right to be Carl's girlfriend.

"There you are."

Carl was standing just off to her left. He was wearing faded jeans, tennis shoes, a white undershirt, and a short-sleeved white oxford-cloth shirt over it. The first two buttons were undone. On his head was the same baseball cap he seemed to constantly wear. He was holding a dark gray backpack over one shoulder. He looked so . . . so English, it almost took her breath away.

But at least his appearance served to remind her that she really didn't know him anymore. Their ties were from long ago.

"Were you looking for me?"

"Ah, yeah. By the time I realized you were in the coffee shop, you'd already run out."

"Why did you care if I was there or not?"

His brow wrinkled. "Hey, may I sit down next to you?"

May wished she had a reason to tell him no, but she didn't. "If you want to sit, then you may. There's room."

"*Danke*." He carefully set his backpack on the ground as he claimed half the bench.

Nee, almost two thirds of it.

Carl was so close, she could smell the soap on his skin . . . and something like a mixture of evergreen and sandalwood. The scent claimed her senses and made her want to lean a little closer. It was disconcerting.

"You're wearing cologne?"

"Aftershave. Why?"

"No reason," she said quickly. Why had she even brought that up?

"I guess I've gotten used to using aftershave balm. It's hard enough to shave around the scar tissue. The balm seems to help."

"You didn't want to grow a beard?"

"To cover up the scars? No. The hair doesn't grow evenly."

"I didn't mean that you needed to cover up your face. I just thought it might be easier on your skin."

"Oh. It ain't." He seemed to think about it for a moment,

then added, "Besides, I might not be Amish, but having a beard while I'm still single doesn't sit right with me."

"I see."

Carl kicked out his legs. "I always liked this creek." He glanced her way. "I used to fish here with Kevin in the summer. Did you come here a lot when we were younger, too? I don't remember seeing you."

"I never came. I discovered it a couple of years ago. A widow donated this bench. I've come here more often since it arrived."

"I bet. This is nice."

Their conversation would've been nice, too. If they were close friends. But they weren't, so this casual chitchat felt artificial.

"Carl, why did you run after me?"

"I wanted to explain about Wendy."

"Who?"

"Oh. The woman I was on the call with. You know, on my computer. We were on a Zoom meeting."

She had no idea what that was, of course. "Your Zoom meeting isn't any of my business. And neither is Wendy."

"Sorry. I thought you might be interested to know that she works for my company. One of my jobs is to help her with her accounts. That's why we were on the Zoom. She wanted to show me some notes and plans for the project she's working on."

She'd gotten it all wrong. "You two seemed to be joking around. I thought you were friends."

"We are, but work friends. Not, you know, social friends." He cast her a sideways look. "I just wanted you to know that. In case you thought she was something else to me."

She could either be honest or salvage her pride. "I did. But like I said earlier, it's not any of my business."

"What were you doing in the shop?"

"I was going to get some coffee, but I changed my mind."

Carl stuffed his hands in his pockets. "Hey, May . . . do you think we'll ever get to the point where we can act like the fire never happened? Where we can just forget about the past?"

Unable to help herself, she gazed at the lines of scars on his left arm. Some were fainter than others, but all were evident. Even after six years. "*Nee.*"

"Wow. Okay."

He was hurt. "I'm not trying to be mean, but the fact is that it did happen, and it's my fault you were burned so badly. I'm glad you don't hate me, but I can't stop carrying the blame on my shoulders. I certainly can't pretend it didn't happen."

"That baggage you're lugging around is going to get heavy."

It already was. "Then I guess I'd better get stronger arms, right?"

He smiled. "Or maybe not try to carry it all on your own."

Those words hit home. "Hey, I heard you know about Walker and Ally."

"Know what?"

"They're in love." There was no other way to say it. When Carl's expression looked pinched, she added, "Walker got mad at all of us last night. He feels that everyone in our family has spent entirely too much time and attention on me. He doesn't like that our families don't get along and that he and Ally have had to sneak around."

Carl frowned. "I feel bad about that, too. Though I don't like her sneaking around at night."

"Walker doesn't like it either."

"It must not bother him too much, though. Otherwise he would've stopped that nonsense."

She looked down at her feet. "I kind of feel the same way, but it's not as if I have any right to tell Walker how to act."

"I haven't broached the subject again since I found Ally sneaking in her bedroom window. I should probably bring it up again."

"If you do, I hope you sound nicer than you do right now. You sound like you're mad."

He stiffened. "I'm not mad—I just hate that our parents are making everything so difficult." He exhaled. "And . . . I really wish she wasn't choosing to meet her boyfriend in the middle of the night. That ain't right, you know?"

"Oh, I know." She had to giggle about that. "But it's her relationship—not yours, right?"

"Of course, but their actions affect more than just my sister and your brother."

"If you say so."

He stood up. "I'm confused. Why are you okay with them being a couple?"

"Because it doesn't matter if I approve or not. It's already happened."

"We'll see about that."

She watched him walk off, his stride so forceful and intent. She'd be more upset about his high-handed manner if she wasn't so sure that he was about to get a run for his money. Walker wasn't going to change his mind about Ally—no matter what Carl had to say to him.

And as for Ally? May was pretty sure that Ally was going to be just as annoyed as Walker if Carl decided to get involved in her relationship.

And that might even be an understatement.

Chapter 13

It was five o'clock, almost supper time. That meant Ally was doing what she always did—hurrying to get all the side dishes finished and placed into her mother's favorite serving dishes.

From there, Kevin—and now Carl, too—would help her put all the serving dishes on the table. Then, at ten minutes after five, the family would wash their hands, gather at the table, and enjoy the meal together.

Just as they'd always done.

Just as her parents did, and their parents, too.

Tonight, they were having smothered pork chops, mashed potatoes, slow-cooked green beans, Watergate salad, and stewed apples. It was a feast and smelled so good.

Her mother's arthritis wasn't acting up, so she'd made a lot of the dinner. Ally did most of the chopping and peeling, but it was a pleasure, since her mother was in a chatty, happy mood.

It was afternoons like this when she felt completely satisfied with her life. She wasn't changing the world, but she didn't need to be. She was a help to her mother and was able to put a fine meal on the table without a tremendous amount of fuss. That was something to be proud of.

"Do you need any help carrying serving dishes to the table?" Kevin asked.

"You may take the potatoes and salad in."

"On it. Carl was behind me in the bathroom. He said to tell you he'd be down in five minutes."

"*Danke.*"

"The pork chops are ready to go out, Al," Mamm said.

"Yes, Mamm." On her way to the table, she saw Carl. He looked pensive.

"Is there more to put out?" he asked.

"Yes. Apples and beans."

"I got the beans," Kevin called out.

"Just the apples, then."

"Okay." Stepping to the side, he motioned for her to stop. "Uh, Ally?"

"Yes?"

"Walker told his parents last night."

She was so glad her hands were free. "Are you sure?"

"Yep. I saw May in town. She told me Walker lost his temper and told his parents that he was in love with you."

She pressed her hands to her face. "Tell me you're joking."

"I can't, Ally. So, tonight's the night to tell Mamm and Daed."

She bit her lip, but nodded.

"It will be okay."

She didn't think it was going to be okay at all, but she also knew she had no choice in the matter. May, Walker, Marjorie, and Ben weren't going to keep their secret forever.

Returning to the kitchen, she hurried to her mother's side—but her father was already there. He had his hand around their mother's waist and was murmuring something sweet and low to her. When her mother laughed in response, her expression softened. For a split second, she looked like a young girl. No doubt like the woman their father had fallen in love with.

Touched by the intimate moment, Ally stood frozen.

"Ally, you may pour water into the glasses," Daed said. He pointed to the full glass pitcher.

She picked it up and carried it to the table. Kevin and Carl were already there, laughing about something. Quickly, she poured each glass half full of water and then sat down, just as Daed escorted their mother to the table.

They were still smiling at each other, which was so nice to see . . . but how long would this happy moment last? For once, both of her parents were in a good mood, she wasn't exhausted, Carl was home, and the meal looked delicious.

Why did tonight have to be the night to share her news?

"Let us all give thanks for the food we are about to receive."

As she'd done for every night of her life, Ally bowed her head and quietly gave thanks—and then added a little prayer that the Lord would watch over them and that the whole night wasn't going to get horrible.

"Ally, would you pass the pork chops when you are ready?" Kevin asked.

"Sure." She speared one, placed it on her plate, and drizzled gravy over it before passing the platter to Kevin on her right.

From her left came the bowl of mashed potatoes. She put a dollop on the plate, then passed it on again.

On and on the five of them went. It was almost as if they were clockwork figures moving in unison. "Carl, sometimes it feels like you never left."

"During moments like this, I feel the same way."

"What do you eat at home? Do you cook a lot?" Kevin asked. "Or do you go out to eat all the time? Do you go to McDonalds and Chipotle?"

"Goodness, boy. Carl canna answer four questions at once."

"Sorry."

"*Nee*, it's no bother to answer you. Let's see, I eat at home most nights, but not like this. Usually I grill chicken or a piece of steak and eat it with a potato and broccoli."

"Do you have a lot of friends from work?" Mamm asked. "I just realized that I never asked."

"I do. We get together from time to time. I have met some guys from church."

"Oh, *jah*. You're on the basketball team, right?"

"It's hardly that. There's an open game every Thursday night. I play with them once or twice a month. Sometimes we go out for chicken wings after."

"You've made a good life for yourself, Carl," Daed said. His expression was filled with pride and approval.

"I've been blessed. It's a blessing to have the opportunity to follow one's dreams. Right, Ally?"

She just about choked on her bite of Watergate salad. "*Jah*."

When Carl continued to stare at her meaningfully, Ally knew that the time had come to at last put everything out in the open. Her heart was pounding as she set her fork down. "Mamm, Daed, Kevin, I have something to tell you. You see, Carl just gave me the opportunity to share something with you all."

"And what is that?" Mamm asked.

"Well, um, it's about Walker Schott."

Daed put his fork and knife down on the table. "What about him?"

Oh, she felt like a worm inching across a crowded side-walk. She was about to get stepped on. Glancing at Carl, he nodded. She supposed she might as well get it over with. "Walker and I have been seeing each other in private for some time. We have fallen in love."

"What?" Kevin asked. "Really?"

"Really."

"Wait, how did Carl know?"

"I saw May Schott in town today. We started talking, and she told me that Walker told her family last night."

Ally was thankful when Carl didn't relay that she'd confided in him two nights earlier. "After Carl told me that, I figured I should tell you all so you wouldn't hear our news from someone else."

"What news?" Daed scoffed. "I don't know what you think is going to happen, but you're mistaken. Nothing is going to happen—beyond you being punished for disobeying me."

Though she could've bet money that her father would react this way, his words still hurt. To her surprise, they also made her stronger. "I'm too old to be punished."

"Oh no, you aren't. You live here, and you are my daughter. We will discuss this later."

"I think we should discuss it now," Carl said. "Ally is right. She is far too old to wait for a punishment, especially since she's done nothing wrong."

"Carl, you are overstepping yourself," Mamm said.

"I don't think so. I am speaking the truth. Ten minutes ago, we were all enjoying our dinner together. The only thing that's changed is that now we all know about Ally and Walker Schott."

Kevin chuckled. "I hate to say it, but Carl's right . . . though you shouldn't have been sneaking around, Al."

"I didn't have a choice. Neither Walker nor I had a choice."

"You did have a choice, Ally," her father corrected. "You could have abided by our rules."

"If you're referring to the 'Don't talk to the Schott family rule,' it was a bad one, especially since you made it up all on your own, Daed."

"Ally, stop," Mamm said.

"Stop what?"

"You are acting as if you haven't been behaving badly. When have you been sneaking out to see Walker?"

"At night."

"Unchaperoned, no doubt."

Carl groaned. "Mamm, don't act like you're shocked. She couldn't have a chaperone if you didn't want her seeing Walker in the first place."

"Ally, you must cut things off," Mamm blurted.

"Why?"

"You know why. Look at your brother. It's May Schott's fault he's like this."

"It is not, and I'm not a victim," Carl said. "I was burned, but now I'm healed."

"I'm not going to stop seeing Walker, Mamm. We're in love."

"Not while you live in my *haus*," her *daed* said.

"So you're going to kick me out?"

"I don't want to, but I will be forced to do what I must if you continue to ignore my wishes."

Ally swallowed. Her father's words weren't a surprise, but they were a disappointment. She'd hoped time—and Carl's reappearance in their lives—would have given him a new perspective and maybe even softened some of his feelings.

Obviously, that wasn't the case. Forcing herself not to think about how empty she'd feel away from her family, she looked directly at her father. "What are you going to do about Mamm when I'm gone?"

His eyes narrowed. "You are actually considering this?"

"You've given me no choice."

"Wait, what about me?" Mamm interrupted.

"Don't worry, Robin. I won't let her leave you."

Still looking offended, her mother folded her arms across her chest. "I am doing just fine. I might let Ally help out a bit here and there, but I can still manage my own *haus*."

Ally was irritated and hurt. She did so much for both of her parents, and now her father was acting as if she didn't matter, and her mother was full-out lying about how much help she provided.

"I'm sorry, Mother, but we both know you are telling a fib."

And just like that, an arctic chill permeated the room.

"Ally," Kevin whispered. "You canna say that."

She didn't want to pretend that her feelings didn't matter or that she didn't have a right to an opinion. "*Nee*, I'm not going to stop. I made most of this meal. I prepared the majority of the dishes. I gathered eggs, washed them, tended the garden, and did two loads of laundry. Tomorrow I will do the same thing, plus accompany Mamm to the market. This isn't anything new, either. I do most of the chores all the time. If I'm not here, they won't get done."

Her mother paled. "Allison."

"I'm sorry, Mamm. I don't want to embarrass you, but I surely don't want to continue to act as if I don't do anything around this house." When no one said another word, Ally knew she couldn't stay there another moment. She got up. "You know, Daed, it's a real shame that your pride is more important than my happiness. But at least I now know where I stand." She tossed her napkin on her plate and walked to her room.

"Where are you going, Ally?" Mamm called out.

"To pack. Daed is right. It really is time I left." Her vision blurred, but she didn't allow the tears to fall.

She was going to have to leave, but at least she'd kept some of her pride.

It seemed she valued pride, too.

Chapter 14

His sweet, so-in-love, beautiful sister had left the table and was likely gathering all of her things together in her room.

Looking around the table, Carl felt dismayed. Kevin seemed subdued but was eating again. His mother was wiping her eyes but didn't say a word. And his father appeared to be completely stunned.

None of them, however, seemed to be getting ready to go after Ally.

That made him so mad. He was very aware of how much Ally did for the family. She shouldn't be kicked out for falling in love.

He got to his feet. "Daed, I don't know what has gotten into you, but I couldn't be more disappointed."

"Don't go to her. She needs to learn."

"Oh, I think she's already learned plenty about where she stands in this house."

"She's been sneaking out. There's no telling what she and that Walker have been doing at night."

Carl felt like rolling his eyes. "You can act horrified because she's been alone with a man in the dark, but we all know that it's the person she's been with that you're really upset about."

"Of course, it is. You should be, too."

"Why?"

"You're scarred because of that family! You had to leave Apple Creek because of the Schotts!"

"I was burned because a wooden barn was hit by lightning in the middle of a thunderstorm. I was burned because it burst into flames like a stack of kindling. The Schotts had nothing to do with it."

"It was the Schotts' barn."

"*Jah, it was.* There was only one reason I was there, and it was because I wanted to see May. My being there was my choice."

"She lured you."

"*Nee.* That's not how it was. I wanted to meet her there. I was on her property so I could see her."

"And the Lord struck that barn with lightning."

"Now you're suggesting that God was involved, too?" Carl shook his head. "I hope and pray that one day you'll realize your anger doesn't have anything to do with me or the Schott family. You can't blame my scars, my leaving Apple Creek, or May when she was only a sixteen-year-old girl. It happened. There is no reason lightning hit our barn or that the fire burned fast or that I got burned. It just did."

"You are putting words in my mouth."

"Well, you certainly can't go blaming Ally and Walker. This rift between our families is your doing. It's all on you."

Mamm inhaled sharply. "Carl, you are still our son. You may not speak to your father that way."

"It's too late for you to declare that we all need to be kind and respectful to each other. The two of you made a mockery of that rule." He scooted back his chair, grabbed his plate and silverware, and carried them into the kitchen. Forced himself to take a fortifying breath. Right now, he had to be the person Ally needed him to be. "Lord, please help me," he whispered.

Though he didn't feel a greater sense of peace, he didn't feel quite as frazzled. He was glad of that.

Hurrying upstairs, he tapped on Ally's door. "It's me, Al. Can I come in?"

After a brief pause, she opened the door. "Hey."

A suitcase was open on her bed, and she was folding up a dress. "Carl, I'm so upset."

"I know." He pulled her into his arms for a hug. She immediately rested her forehead on his chest and started crying.

Making him feel even worse. She was just a young girl. A sheltered girl whose whole world was her family, Apple Creek, and Walker Schott. Why hadn't he thought more about the consequences before spouting off his advice?

Feeling even more inept, he patted her back. "I am so sorry for encouraging you to speak up," he murmured when her tears subsided. "I should've kept my mouth shut."

With a ragged sigh, she pulled away. "I wish I could say that Mamm and Daed's reactions were surprising, but they weren't." Looking bitter, she added, "They were as difficult and unyielding as I feared they'd be."

"They sure surprised me."

"You've been gone. I think your memories of Daed's stubbornness have faded."

"Maybe so." He watched her fold another dress and place it in her suitcase. "Where will you go?"

She shrugged. "I have no idea."

Thinking quickly, he said, "I can either find you an Airbnb nearby or a hotel. Which would you prefer?"

"I've never stayed by myself before. I don't know." She lowered her voice. "I don't have any money either."

"I'm paying for it. And I'll stay with you." Deciding to make it easier on her, he added, "I'm going to find us a two-bedroom place on Airbnb."

"You don't mind?" The gratitude in her expression broke his heart. She shouldn't have to be grateful for his support; she should expect it.

"Ally, of course I don't mind. Besides, this whole mess is my fault. I pushed you to tell Mamm and Daed about your relationship with Walker."

"You might have pushed, but it was necessary. I needed to come clean."

"Everything needed to be out in the open, but you didn't have to do it so abruptly. Why, I practically prodded you at the dinner table to tell them everything."

She didn't respond as she moved to her dresser and added more items to her suitcase.

Glad his phone was a hotspot, he clicked a few more buttons. "Okay, I'm online. I'll find us a place, pack up a bag, and be ready in fifteen minutes. Will that be enough time for you?"

She nodded. "I don't want to be here one minute longer than I have to."

She looked so distraught, he felt even worse. "I am sorry, Ally. I'll find a way to make this right. Try not to worry."

Ally didn't say anything, but what could she say, anyway? That it was okay? It was so very far from that.

Fuming at himself, he walked down the hall and sat on the edge of his twin bed. With a heavy heart, he began flipping through the app, looking for a place to stay where Ally would feel comfortable.

When his door opened, he barely looked up. "Sorry, Al. I've—"

"It isn't Ally."

It sure wasn't. It was his mother. Finally looking up, he met her eyes. She had the same bluish-gray eyes that he and Ally did. At the moment, they looked luminescent, thanks to her unshed tears.

"Mamm?"

"*Jah.*" She remained in the doorway, her hand braced on the doorframe. Carl wondered if she was using the wood as support—or to help her refrain from walking into his room.

When another minute passed without her saying anything, he pulled out the duffel bag he'd brought. He'd stored it under the bed.

"You're packing a bag?"

"Yes."

"Why? Are you intending to leave with Ally?"

He loved his mother, but he didn't have a lot of patience at the moment for such silly questions. "Of course I am. I'm not going to send her out by herself."

She bit her lip. "Did you put her up to this?"

"I suppose I did. Walker's already told his parents that he intends to marry Ally. I figured you would rather hear the news from your daughter instead of one of your women friends. I was obviously wrong."

She flinched. "You don't have to be so harsh, son."

"I reckon I don't. But then, neither do you or Daed."

"He's very angry."

"If he is, then he's in good company. I'm angry, too. As is Ally."

"Your father and I are hurt. She's taking sides against us." Waving a hand ineffectually again, she murmured, "Can't you see how this secret romance of hers makes us feel?"

"I think you should be feeling embarrassed that she had to sneak around in the first place." He turned to face her.

"Mamm, you know Walker Schott is a *gut* man. He has a good job and is as solid as they come. More important, he loves Ally. Isn't that what counts?"

"Love isn't the most important thing, Carl."

"That's where you're wrong. I think it is the most important thing. Love is what gets a person through hardships. Love keeps one from feeling lonely. Love gives a person hope for the future. Without love, everything in this life pales."

"That's romantic language. But you'll learn the truth one day."

"I hope I don't learn your truth then. Now I've got to go."

"Carl, please stay. I just got you back."

"When you and Daed apologize to Ally and ask her to come home—and when it's okay for Walker to come courting—then I'll come back with her."

She wrung her hands, acting as if he'd just asked her to give him the moon. "I don't know if that day will ever come."

"Then I hope you enjoy your solitude, Mamm. Excuse me, I need to get my things out of the bathroom."

Walking right past her was hard. But it wasn't the hardest thing he'd ever done.

What his mother didn't seem to realize was that the reason he could talk so knowledgeably about love was because he'd experienced it himself, once upon a time.

Six years ago, he'd had something special with an amazing girl. His love for her had made him feel foolish, do risky things . . . push the boundaries their parents had set. He'd done so many wrong things so very willingly. All because May had loved him just as much.

Yeah. He absolutely knew what it was like to risk so much just to have a chance at happiness.

Because of that, he also knew the consequences of ignoring those feelings or pretending they weren't one of the Lord's greatest gifts. When one did that, all the color in the world faded to gray.

He knew it all too well because once he'd had so much. Then, like a stubborn fool, he'd also thrown it all away.

Chapter 15

May was so proud of her girls. Her trio of two-year-old alpacas had behaved brilliantly with the ladies group from the nearby Mennonite church. The women had reached out to her, asking if they could have an outing at the Shotts' barn and possibly even get their pictures taken with some of the animals.

The amount they'd offered to pay was generous, and so she'd agreed immediately. Only later did she start to wonder if she'd made a mistake. Some folks were disappointed when her alpacas weren't as outgoing or affectionate as they'd hoped. Then, too, there were the girls' moods. Sometimes they simply weren't in the mood to perform their tricks, which was frustrating to May and a disappointment to anyone who paid to see them.

She'd learned to give people low expectations so they wouldn't be disappointed if her alpacas simply wanted to eat their hay.

Today, however, the girls had all rung bells, and Cupid had sat down when May asked—the newest trick.

Dancer had even been willing to get her picture taken with all the women. It was an adorable scene. The women had cooed and complimented her. It was as if Dancer understood every word and preened with happiness.

So, that had been wonderful. It had given her a real sense of satisfaction to see the fruits of all her hard work with the alpacas. She only wished Walker had been there, too.

She'd just put on her oldest dress and was mucking stalls when her brother arrived on his bicycle. He looked troubled and tired. May would've been more concerned about him if she hadn't just had to do both the tour and all the barn chores alone. Impatiently, she waited for him to apologize.

As he took his time putting away the bike and still barely looked at her, May felt some of her anger fade. Had something happened? He was acting very peculiar. "Walker, aren't you going to say something?"

"Hmm?" He blinked, as if he had to remember what she was even talking about. "Oh, *jah*. I'm sorry I wasn't here this morning. How did it go?"

"The girls were great. I wish you could've seen them— Dancer was attentive and focused. She rang the bells, then encouraged Cupid and Dasher to do the same. I'm really proud of them."

"That certainly is gut news." His blue eyes warmed, though his expression was still troubled. "I wish I had been here to see it."

Something really bad must have happened. Stepping closer, May curved her hand around his arm. "Walker, what happened? Where have you been all day?"

He pursed his lips. "I was with Ally and Carl," he said at last.

"You went to the Hiltys' *haus*?"

"Not at all. As of last night, Ally and Carl are staying in Ira Jensen's old *haus*, which he made into an Airbnb."

"Oh, my word. What happened?"

He stuffed his hands in his pockets. "Just about every-thing. Ally was too upset to tell me the whole story, but essentially, Carl had heard from you that I'd told our parents about me and Ally. Carl encouraged Ally to come clean with their parents. She did so last night at supper."

Her stomach sank. "And let me guess, they didn't take it well."

"Not even a little bit. Ally said her *daed* got really mad, and even Robin did, too."

"Oh, no."

"Then things got even worse. Their father barely waited a beat before giving Ally an ultimatum—end everything with me or leave the house. They left last night."

She felt as if a rock was lodged in her throat. "I'm so sorry. I . . . I feel like this is my fault."

"I said the same thing to her and Carl." Walker laughed dryly. "Actually, even Carl tried to take the blame. I guess he encouraged Ally to tell her parents that she and I had been sneaking around together, thinking that they were going to learn the truth sooner or later. He was right."

"I agree."

"I knew they wouldn't be happy, but I never imagined they'd kick Ally and Carl out at night."

Walker's expression turned fierce. "Oh, it wasn't like that. May, Able didn't kick out both Ally and Carl. Just Ally. If Carl hadn't stood up for his sister, Able and Robin would've let Ally leave by herself at night."

May gasped. "Where would she have gone?"

"Over here, I guess." Walker blinked, obviously attempting to rein in his emotions. "I am so angry with them, I can hardly talk about it."

"I don't blame you. I'm angry, too. Poor Ally!"

"Ally told me that Carl gave their parents a piece of his

mind. He let them know that he thought they were being terrible, focusing on pride instead of family and love."

May nodded. She could absolutely imagine Carl saying such things. He'd always been the type of man to speak his mind. But she had a feeling he was as devastated by the events as Ally and Walker were. "So now they're in the Jensens' rental *haus*?"

"*Jah*. For at least a couple of nights. Until Ally decides when she wants to go home with Carl."

Home? It took a second to connect the dots. "You mean Cleveland?"

He waved a hand, as if Ally's move was inevitable. "She doesn't have anywhere else to go."

Stunned, May sat down on an old wooden bench. "Walker, we have got to find a solution."

"There isn't one—not that I can see. Ally is really upset, and Carl is determined to be there for her. She either needs to go with him or break up with me and tell her parents that they were right."

"And continue this feud."

"*Jah*." He sighed. "But we all know that ain't good. Not even our parents want it to continue."

"Did they ever?" May was startled to realize that she didn't even remember whether her parents had understood the Hiltys' blame.

Walker sat down beside her. "I don't know. All I do know is that everything is a big mess. I wish I could move away to be with her."

Her eyes widened. "Walker, you wouldn't move away, would you?"

Looking bleak, he shook his head. "Not only are my life and my job here on the farm and with the alpacas, but I'd have to be English if I went to Cleveland with Ally. That ain't who I am."

May knew what her brother meant. Some folks might think that someone could decide to leave the Old Order and become English on a whim, but the truth was far from that. Every person she knew who had left the faith had said that it was difficult and not without a lot of tears—from both them and their families.

In addition, changing one's entire way of life wasn't easy. The Amish might be aware of the Internet, computers, cell phone plans, and driver's licenses. Becoming used to it all was a much different proposition. One or two of her friends from childhood had left during their *rumspringa* but returned to living Amish when they realized just how different life was on the outside.

"There's got to be another way to resolve everything, Walker."

"Such as?"

"I don't know. Maybe we should get Mamm and Daed involved."

"First, it ain't like Mamm and Daed are all that pleased about Ally and me sneaking around behind their backs."

"They'll get over it. After all, you two have come clean now."

"Even if they were okay with me and Ally, it doesn't matter. Able and Robin are not okay—they've basically disowned their daughter."

The idea made her feel sick to her stomach. "That's so terrible. Maybe our parents can talk to theirs."

Walker shook his head again. "I don't think they'd do that."

Her brother looked so defeated. She figured he had every right to feel down, but she had a nagging feeling that they were missing something. A detail that would make all the difference.

Suddenly, it came to her. It was the most obvious solution. *Nee*, it was the only right thing to do. "Walker, I have the answer."

"Which is?"

"You and Ally need to get married."

He rolled his eyes. "May, that's what I've been trying to tell ya. We can't get married because her parents don't want me courting her."

"Take Robin and Able out of the equation. You've tried to get their blessing, and you've tried to smooth things over with them. If they won't see reason, it's not your fault. You should go to the bishop and Preacher Elias and ask for their help. Then you should try to get married as soon as they say you can."

"May, wait."

"No. Listen, Walker, don't you see? When you're married, you two can live here."

He started to shake his head, then froze. "That might work."

She grinned. "I know!"

"It's going to be difficult, but no more difficult than the other options."

"I agree!"

For the first time since he'd entered the barn, a hint of a smile crossed his face. "Now all I have to do is convince Ally that this is the right thing to do."

"You can do it, Walker." She reached out and clasped his hand. "If Ally was willing to leave her house last night for love, then she'll be willing to talk to the bishop with ya."

He squeezed her hand before standing up. "I hope and pray that you're right."

"Me, too." She kept her voice light, but, in truth, May wasn't sure what was going to happen next.

"Will you come with me?"

"Of course."

"Okay. You fill in Mamm, and I'll go hitch up the buggy."

Standing up, she could practically hear the Lord tell her to take a deep breath. *One step at a time, May. One step at a time.*

She hoped He would continue giving her guidance the rest of the day. She was going to need it.

Chapter 16

The Jensens' rental boasted a very fine backyard. It was fenced and had a spacious Trex deck. Several lounge chairs were arranged on it. In addition, there was a fire pit off to one side of the yard. The Jensens had bought brightly colored Adirondack chairs to surround it. A gas grill and patio set took up another portion of the space.

In addition, the house, though small, was very pretty. There were two bedrooms, one bath, and a modern kitchen with stainless-steel appliances and black granite countertops. There was a fireplace in the living room, Wi-Fi, a flat-screen TV, and a leather sectional.

It was all mighty nice.

Honestly, if the circumstances were different, Carl knew he'd feel like he'd gone on a vacation. He certainly wished his condo in Cleveland was as comfortable and well appointed.

However, since he was sitting in a lounge chair on the back deck with his crying sister, Carl couldn't think of a worse place to be. Why had he ever opened his big mouth?

He hadn't been home, living day-to-day with his parents and siblings, for years. Not since the fire.

In that time, he'd grown up a lot. He'd also started to want different things. No, to expect different things. Some of those expectations—like being listened to in a meeting—made sense.

Others—such as giving relationship advice to Amish courting couples—were woefully misguided and just plain wrong.

"I'm so sorry, Ally," he said for at least the tenth time in the last sixteen hours. "I should've kept my mouth shut."

With a sniff, she raised her chin. "Nee, this wasn't your fault. This blow-up was bound to happen sooner or later. All we did was hasten the argument." She swiped her hand across the tear tracks on her cheeks. "What I can't believe is that it all went so badly. I knew Mamm and Daed would get angry, but I really thought that they'd want to talk about it."

"I thought maybe Mamm would try to calm Daed down. Not back him up."

She nodded. "And then there's Kevin. I know he's only sixteen, but he didn't try to defend me at all." She frowned. "It was as if he was on their side but didn't want to make me mad at him."

Carl had felt the same way. "He surprised me, too. One day I'm going to talk to him about that."

"If we ever talk to him again. It's not like Kevin even gave me a hug goodbye."

"We can't think about that now. Ally, listen to me. I . . . I know you need some time, but we canna stay here for longer than a couple of nights. I can't afford to lose all my savings while we decide what to do next."

"I understand." Her bottom lip trembled. "My head seems to think that I should go back with you for a spell."

"You can certainly do that. Ah, what does your heart say?"

"That if I go so far away, I'm going to miss Walker something awful. I'd feel terrible about leaving Mamm, too. She acts like she doesn't need help, but she does."

Carl feared Ally was right. "Maybe Kevin will step up and help her more."

"He might not have stood up for me, but he does work in the fields with Daed. He's a good farmer."

"You're right. He is."

"Could we maybe stay here at least one more night? In the meantime, I'll get some more of my things."

"Of course. We can do that." He was about to add something more when they heard a knock at the door.

Opening it, he grinned at the sight of Walker and May. "Isn't this a nice surprise!"

"*Danke* for staying someplace close," Walker joked.

"Walker, I'm so glad to see you." Ally rushed to his side.

Carl couldn't help watching the easy way his sister stepped into Walker's arms—and how gentle he was with her.

"Did you really think I wouldn't come back?" Carl murmured.

May met his gaze. It felt as if a thousand words passed between them as he reached for her hands. "I'm glad you came, too," he whispered.

"Walker wanted his visit to be proper this time."

"He didn't trust me to chaperone?" Carl wasn't sure if he should be amused or offended.

"I think it was just an excuse because he wanted some moral support."

"Ally was pretty rattled, too." Deciding there was no need for discretion, he added, "To be honest, I was also. My parents were unyielding."

May peeked at their siblings again. Walker still had his arms wrapped around Ally and was speaking to her in low tones. Ally was gazing up at him and listening intently. "I hope they will be okay."

"Me, too. I'm not sure what to do to make things better,

though." He sighed. "May, I'm so horrified. One would think, after the fire and all my injuries, that my parents would have learned to be thankful for all blessings. Or, at the very least, not act as if two people falling in love was a source of discomfort."

"I feel the same way. But Walker and I did come up with some ideas about how to resolve everything."

"Really? What?"

"Maybe we should all discuss it together?"

Noticing that his sister had moved even closer to Walker, Carl nodded. "*Jah*, that's probably a good idea." Raising his voice, he said, "May was just telling me that you two came up with some ideas to help with this situation. I think the four of us should talk."

Walker nodded. "That's a good idea." He looked around. "Hey, this place is nice."

Ally giggled. "I said the same thing."

Carl shared another amused glance with May. "There's a couch and two chairs in here. Come sit down."

"We bought some bottles of water," May added. "I'll go get four."

Several moments later, they were all sitting together, Carl and May on the couch and Ally and Walker in the chairs. Carl was relieved to see that Ally looked far calmer. To his surprise, he realized that he felt calmer as well. Obviously, it was better for the four of them to join forces instead of trying to do everything on their own. "So, what's your idea?" he asked.

"Well, May and I decided that there are three options for Ally and me. The first is that Ally listens to your parents and she and I don't see each other again."

Ally inhaled sharply. "You think that's an option?"

"It's not my choice," Walker said. "But yes, it is an option."

"The second one is to be patient," May added quickly. "Your parents can't stay mad at our family for the rest of their lives. Plus, we would ask our parents to talk to them."

"That might work," Carl said. "It might take time, but things have to change for the better, especially if our mothers renew their friendship."

"It might take years, though," Walker added. "And I don't want to wait that long."

Some of the excitement shining in Ally's eyes faded. "What's the third option?"

"You should probably explain this one, Walker," May said softly.

"All right." Walker stood up, moved to stand directly in front of Ally, and then blurted, "We should get married right away."

Chapter 17

We should get married right away. Ally couldn't believe Walker had just blurted out that statement, as if he wasn't talking about one of the biggest events of her life.

Of *their* lives.

Maybe that detail didn't matter as much as the fact that he was completely serious. He was truly proposing, and he was truly waiting for an answer. Right then and there.

The statement kept ringing in her ears. Teasing her. Scaring her. It was hard to breathe.

Honestly, Ally felt as if all the air in her body had just been knocked out of her. And maybe it had been. What else could explain the myriad of emotions she was feeling? Shock and excitement and disappointment and fear, all mixed up with a good amount of nausea.

She swallowed hard. Tried to analyze his words.

Yep, she had just gotten a marriage proposal, but it wasn't anything like she'd ever imagined. It wasn't even actually a real proposal. It was more of an announcement, fueled by desperation and need.

The air in the room felt stifling and thick. She darted a look at Walker. He was staring at her intently, silently begging her to respond. May's face was as impassive as a china doll's. Frozen in place.

Finally, Ally looked at Carl. Her older brother looked furious. When she met his gaze, he shook his head. "*Nee.*"

Her Englisher brother, in his jeans and tennis shoes and baseball cap, was now getting involved in her marriage plans? As dismayed as she was by Walker's non-proposal, she was even more irritated by Carl's pronouncement.

"Excuse me?" she asked.

"Come on, Ally. This is not the future you planned on. No way am I going to let you get married in a rush. Everyone is going to think you're with child."

"No one would disrespect her like that," Walker said.

"It doesn't matter if they only disrespect you, the damage would be done." Carl shook his head again. "Nope. It ain't happening."

"Don't tell me what to do, Carl."

"I'm trying to make you see reason," he retorted.

"Demanding a quick marriage isn't the way to solve anything."

Walker groaned. "Ally, I'm not *demanding* that you do anything."

"I'm sorry, but you kind of are," May interjected. "You're not giving Ally any other options."

Ally folded her arms across her chest. "See?"

"May, I really don't think this has to do with anyone except Ally and me," Walker said.

His sister shook her head. "You are wrong. It affects all of us. Obviously."

Ally didn't even know whom to turn to. When she finally looked at her brother, she sighed.

Carl stared at her intently. "I don't want to make you

more upset, but I want you to be sure. So you do want to go get married right away."

"I didn't say that."

May stood up. "Walker, come sit down. You sit down, too, Carl. The four of us need to talk about this reasonably."

"That will be difficult to do, since his suggestion wasn't the least bit reasonable." Carl lowered his voice. "As much as I appreciate your wanting to make things right, marrying in haste ain't the answer."

"For the record, it was my idea," May said. "And it was only an idea. And it's a wedding we're talking about. Not something terrible."

"But that ain't what Ally wants," Carl said.

May rolled her eyes. "Are you sure about that?"

"Stop!" Ally jumped to her feet. "Carl, stop talking and sit down. May, I know you're trying to help, but you're not. And Walker, I . . . I can't believe you finally asked me like that." Pleased that she'd given everyone a piece of her mind, she sat back down and pressed her hands to her face.

Walker knelt on the ground near her feet. "Ally, this might not be the proposal of your dreams. Our wedding might not be the wedding you always wanted, but you can't deny that the end result will make up for the disappointments. We'll be married, and you'll be my wife."

She lowered her hands. "Where would we even live?"

"On our property. In the empty *dawdi haus*. Just like we always planned."

"Your parents would be okay with that?"

After a brief hesitation, he nodded. "They'll have to be."

Feeling even more crestfallen, she moaned. "Walker, they don't know about this plan?"

"Of course, they don't. May and I just thought of it. Besides, I might be making a mess of things, but even I know a man doesn't discuss living arrangements with his parents before talking to the woman he loves." He reached for her hand. "And I do love you, Allison Hilty."

"Oh, Walker." Tears filled her eyes.

Carl stood up again. "Ah, May . . . would you like to go see the backyard? There's a swing."

"I'd love to."

"We're only going to be outside ten minutes, Ally," he warned.

"I understand, *bruder*."

Still kneeling at her feet, Walker smiled at her. "I'm not sure, but I think your brother just gave us his blessing."

She giggled. "I wouldn't go that far, but I do think he's come around. It was shocking, you know."

"I know. I was shocked by the idea, too. I had always planned to ask you while we were on a buggy ride."

"A buggy proposal?"

"Well, not exactly." He reached for her other hand. "I was going to put together a picnic, take you to the banks of Apple Creek, and ask you there." He ran a hand over his face. "Then I was going to tell you that I love you and give you lots of reasons to love me back."

She was starting to think that maybe she didn't need a picnic and buggy ride after all. "Like what?"

"What reasons?"

She giggled. "*Jah*."

Looking earnest, he drew a deep breath. "Well, first, I am a good provider. One might not think there is a lot of money in alpacas, but I do real well. I also will farm my father's land." Obviously warming up to the topic, he added, "Then there's the fact that the *dawdi haus* is plenty nice."

"Is that right?" Like she cared about that. "Is that all?"

"As a matter of fact, *nee*. You see, I am actually very even-keeled. I don't get angry easily, and I don't get flustered. I'm a pleasant companion."

"Good companionship is important, I suppose."

Doubt filled his eyes. "I also don't expect you to wait on me hand and foot. I will help around the house."

"Is that all?"

"*Nee.* I like to do a lot of the same things you do. You and I can have a good, happy life together." He leaned forward. "Of course, there's also one other thing that's in my favor."

"What is that?"

"I not only love you more than you'll ever know, but that love is not going to fade away." He leaned even closer. So close that his breath brushed against her skin. "Then, of course, there's the way you melt for me whenever I kiss you, Ally."

A shiver raced through her. "I don't think you're supposed to mention things like that."

"All right. I won't. I'll just show you . . . If you'll be mine? Do you think you can one day come to love me, too?"

What could she say but the truth? "I love you now."

His gaze warmed. "Will you marry me, Ally?"

There was only one answer to give. It might be foolhardy but she had to listen to her heart. "Yes, Walker. I will."

Walker smiled, then pulled her toward him. Brushed his lips against her jaw before claiming her lips.

And within two very short seconds, she practically forgot her name.

The sliding glass door opened, reminding Walker where they were—and that they most definitely weren't alone. "Did you need something, Carl?"

"Oh, yeah. I need to make sure that you two are engaged," Carl said.

Finally standing up, Walker pulled her to her feet. "May and Carl, Ally said yes. She's agreed to be my wife and make me the happiest man in the county. Please wish us well."

Chapter 18

Looking out the window of the Airbnb while Walker drove Ally to the Shotts' house in the buggy, May felt at loose ends. No, it was a bit more than that—she was stunned.

The Lord had certainly taken a hand in the last two hours' events, there was no doubt about that. When she and Walker had first decided to visit Ally and Carl, it was to offer their support and present a couple of ideas. She'd imagined she and Walker would discuss various options as to what Ally and Walker could do in the future—and then that Carl and Ally would ignore them all. Or, in the best-case scenario, Ally would ask Walker to talk with her about their ideas.

But now, here she was, sitting in an Airbnb with Carl, while their siblings drove off into the sunset, obviously as happy as clams.

"I can't believe what just happened," she murmured. "Did that just take you off guard, too?"

"Yes."

"I can't believe they're now engaged, and our parents aren't even talking."

"If I drank, I do believe I'd be popping open a beer right now," Carl replied. "Ally's and Walker's romance is wearing me out."

Turning from the window, she smiled at him. "I've been feeling the same way."

He stood up, giving her a good view of what he was wearing—a snug-fitting, gray T-shirt, faded army green chinos, and flip-flops. He looked so English, so effortlessly casual and handsome, sometimes she couldn't help but stare.

He gestured toward the door. "Want to go sit outside on the back patio for a spell? You don't need to go home yet, do you?"

"I'd love to sit outside." She laughed softly. "There's no way I want to go home right now."

"I'm so glad. I'm not up for going to either of our houses just yet—or seeing my sister and her fiancé."

"I'm pretty sure they don't want to see us either," she joked.

"Come on then. Let's go relax. Grab a soda from the fridge if you want," he said as he led the way outside.

May grabbed a soda and followed him out. There was a nice deck with a table and chair set made of treated wood. Bright orange cushions decorated the chairs. She took the one to Carl's right.

"What do you think your parents are going to say when they get to your house?" Carl asked while she took a fortifying sip of lemon-lime soda.

A couple of scenarios came to mind, some better than others. "I'm not sure. Hopefully, they'll just be happy for Walker and Ally and allow them to enjoy the moment."

"But?"

"But I think that's doubtful. I'm sure my *mamm* will either start making wedding plans or my father will want to give Ally and Walker a tour of the *dawdi haus*—just as if

Walker hasn't been in there a dozen times before." Thinking about how excited her parents would be, she said, "Actually, I think both of those things will happen."

"That's it? You don't expect them to raise a fuss?"

"*Nee.* Walker was adamant about his love for your sister when he announced their relationship at supper. My parents are pretty good at picking their battles, but it's not exactly an issue anyway. Your parents and mine might not want to talk to each other, but there's no denying that my parents like Ally very much. It's a *gut* match."

"I wish mine were as giving and open-minded. I tell you what, May, I couldn't believe how easily they let Ally leave the house. I'm a little ashamed of the way they acted." He pressed his lips together. "No, make that really ashamed."

She knew she'd feel the same way . . . but also felt that Carl's taking responsibility for their actions wasn't going to help the situation. "You can't take their behavior on your shoulders," May said quickly. "It's on them."

"But what if they don't see reason soon?"

"I don't know. I guess Ally and Walker will get married, they'll live in the *dawdi haus* on our property, and your parents will decide either to be mad or deal with it."

"I don't think it's going to be as cut-and-dried as that." Carl looked upset.

"What do you want to happen?"

"I don't know." Stretching his arms above his head, he chuckled softly. "I guess I want life to start being easier." Darting a look her way, he winced. "I realize this isn't about me. I'm being selfish."

"Ally's situation does affect you, though. Right? It affects all of us." Softly, she added, "That's one thing I've learned during all this time—just because something happens to someone else, if I care about that person, it affects me, too."

"I guess it does, to an extent."

Here was her chance. She could either bring up how she felt after he left or keep it to herself a little while longer.

But hadn't she kept all these feelings in for far too long already?

She sipped her drink, then said, "Carl, when you got so badly burned and were hospitalized for months, you never allowed me to come see you. That was really hard for me." When she noticed his expression tighten, she rushed to continue. "And I don't mean it was hard in comparison to your life—because we both know there was no comparison between my disappointment and the pain you were going through."

She pressed her hands on the surface of the picnic table. "What I'm trying to say is that we'd been really good friends, and then we, ah, kissed . . . and then you were gone. Losing you was very hard."

His expression tightened. To May's surprise, the movement caused some of the scars on his face to stand out more than usual. It was the first time since he'd arrived that she'd even noticed the damaged skin.

Carl appeared to be weighing his words carefully. When he spoke, his voice sounded flat, almost strained. "May, I promise you did not want to see me during those first six months after the fire. I wasn't in a good place. Most of the time I didn't even know where I was."

"Carl, don't you think I was worried about you? Don't you understand that all I wanted to do was be there for you? I didn't need anything from you other than to be by your side."

"The abrading of my skin and the treatments and the grafts . . . every day was filled with varying degrees of pain. I wasn't kind or nice to anyone." He swallowed. "I cried a lot."

"Carl."

He swallowed again. "What I'm trying to say is that I didn't have anything left over. I wouldn't have been nice. I didn't have the energy to be near anyone. I didn't even want my mother near me."

"But what about after?"

"After I got out of the hospital?"

"Yes. What about when I tried to see you while you were in that rehabilitation clinic? I called, and the receptionist said patients could receive visitors, but you still didn't want to see me. Why? Was it because you blamed me?" Forcing herself to get a grip, she inhaled. "No, let me do this right. Carl, is the reason your parents blame me for the fire because you've blamed me, too?"

"I don't blame you."

"Did you used to?"

"May, what does it matter?"

"It matters because this rift between our two families has torn us all up. It matters because we never talked about any of it. Did you?"

"I don't know. Maybe I did. You wouldn't move, May. The fire was spreading; stuff was falling down from the rafters; I was scared to death; but you wouldn't move." He closed his eyes. "I thought we were going to die in that barn."

She swallowed. "All right."

"Do you hate me now?"

"*Nee.* Of course not. Besides, I'm not remembering it any different. I wanted to move and run out. But I was frozen in place."

Carl made a noise deep in his throat. "Do you feel any better now? Because I sure don't."

She couldn't help but laugh, though it was dry and strained-sounding. The opposite of any sort of happy noise. "Maybe I do. I've carried a lot of guilt with me all this time."

"I carried guilt, too. I knew better than to meet you in that barn. I knew, after all our weeks of circling around each other, what was going to happen if we ever got the chance to be completely alone." The muscle in his jaw flinched. "I knew I wouldn't be able to stop myself from kissing you."

"I kissed you back."

"I know." His eyes lit up. "After all this time . . . after all these years that have gone by . . . the memory is still vivid. I mean, it is for me."

"It is for me, too. While I regret being so scared that I couldn't move . . . I don't regret that kiss, Carl."

"That would be *kisses*, May," he corrected. "We shared far more than one chaste kiss."

Even after all these years, the memory of that stolen moment still made her skin flush. Determined to show him that she was no longer a timid young girl, she looked directly in his eyes. "You're right. It was a lot more. But as much as I regret how I acted when the fire broke out, I don't regret what we did. I never have."

"I've never regretted it either."

The intense way he was looking at her made May's pulse race. It made her wonder if everything that had been between them wasn't lost after all. "At least we agree on that," she said.

Looking pleased, he nodded. "That is true." His cell phone rang. "Sorry, it could be wor—hello? Yes? Ah, yes, Daed. May and I were with them. They're at the Schotts' farm now." After another pause, Carl's distinctive gray-blue eyes met hers. "What are they doing? Well, I reckon they're telling Marjorie and Ben Schott that they're going to be living in the *dawdi haus* over there. Walker and Ally mean to marry right away. With or without your and Mamm's support."

May pressed a hand over her mouth. She wasn't sure whether she was shocked by the way Carl matter-of-factly shared the news, amused by his almost bored look at his father's answering rant . . . or a strange combination of both.

It seemed another secret was out in the open. And like that burning fire . . . the only way to survive the consequences was to get out of the way or get burned.

Chapter 19

It was a day that would go down in history. Maybe not for everyone, but certainly for Walker and everyone he cared about. Less than three hours after he and Ally took an awkward tour of the Schotts' *dawdi haus* with his father, Carl and May arrived with the news that everyone was invited to the Hiltys' for some dessert and coffee. Everyone was expected to go, since Preacher Elias would be there, too.

He whispered to Ally that he was fairly sure Elias had shown up so that their parents didn't try to maim each other.

As they all stood in the same room for the first time in six years, he knew his mother was about to cry. Not out of sadness but because she was happy. "It's been too long, Robin," she whispered.

Robin looked taken aback, but then something seemed to click inside her. "I agree," she whispered. They went to the kitchen to pour coffee for everyone. Then they all sat in the Hiltys' large basement, where Preacher Elias discussed marriage plans with them.

Walker was surprised at how easily Elias accepted their spur-of-the-moment nuptials.

"Everyone in Apple Creek knows the two of you are supposed to be together. I think it's time you stopped worrying about pleasing your parents. The Lord knows what's in your heart, and I'm certain He feels that it's well and good."

Walker still wasn't sure how Ally's parents had gone from kicking her out to taking her back in, but that's what they did. Ally shrugged when he shared that he was worried about her staying there. "It's just for two weeks."

Walker was pretty sure that he was going to be saying those same words to himself over and over during the next fourteen days.

When it was time for everyone to go, no one would call their two families' relationship cordial, but it did seem better. At least their fathers didn't seem to actively hate each other anymore.

All too soon, Preacher Elias was ushering them out the door. "I know you'll be missing Ally, Walker, but we don't want to wear out our welcome. Ain't so?"

Walker wasn't sure if Elias was joking or not. "I guess not," he mumbled when it was obvious the preacher was looking for his confirmation.

"That's what I wanted to hear." Turning to the rest of the gathering, he raised a hand as he walked to his rig. "See you all on Sunday!"

After a few more parting words, he and his family started for home.

It hadn't been easy for Walker to let her stay there without him. Though, of course, Ally wouldn't have appreciated the way he phrased that. To her mind, she was doing what she needed to do—and there was no such thing as Walker "letting" her do anything.

Of course she was right. He admired Ally's bright mind and strong will. That said, saying goodbye and walking home with his sister and parents had been one of the hardest moments of his life.

"This is for the best," Daed said. "If you and Ally intend to marry in two weeks, she needs to reestablish some semblance of a relationship with her parents."

"I know, but she looked miserable."

"I think she looked more determined than anything," May said. "When Robin chided her for doing things out of order, Ally barely pretended to listen. I bet she's going to count the days until she's Walker's wife."

"I know I am," Walker said.

His father chuckled. "If you didn't, I would worry about you. I know you're concerned about your fiancée, but one hopes that every bridegroom is eager to tie the knot." He winked, signaling that Walker was likely eager for more than just reciting vows.

"Ugh," May whispered.

Walker chuckled. If there was anything guaranteed to make his sister feel uncomfortable, he reckoned it was their father talking about eager brides and grooms.

Deciding it was a good idea to move the conversation along, Walker returned to his original concern. "I really am worried about how Robin and Able are going to treat her."

"She has Carl there," May said. "Carl told me he isn't going to move back until Ally is safely married."

"You two sure have gotten close, May." Mamm smiled. "Perhaps we'll soon be planning your wedding, too."

"I don't know about that, Mamm."

"You and Carl have gotten closer since his return, don'tcha think?" Walker asked. He actually thought they were just as serious about each other as he and Ally were . . . May and Carl just weren't ready to admit it yet.

"We're talking now, and we share a lot of history."

"But nothing more?" Mamm asked.

"I'm not sure. We . . . um, we're different than Walker and Ally. We've been apart, he's English now . . . and we'll always have that fire between us."

Their father slowed his steps until May caught up to him. "May, I'm going to tell you the same thing I told Robin and Able. I've always figured life is made up of a lot of events, some big and some small."

"I agree."

"Do you also agree that some of those events—like weddings and funerals and births—well, they're going to be memorable because they are huge, life-changing events?"

"*Jah.*"

"Then I want you to think about how the Lord gives us all a myriad of other less-significant moments in our lives. Some of them create lasting memories, too, for one reason or another. But I've always felt that there are other events that mark a person in unique ways. Whether it's a fire or a job loss or even an injury, tragedy strikes each of us. And those things don't affect all of us the same way."

He exhaled. "What I'm trying to tell ya is that every person on this earth has their own 'fire' story. Maybe it doesn't involve getting burned or separated from someone they care for, but it's a trauma. I think it's wrong to put so much emphasis on just one event—and selfish to think everyone else hasn't gone through something just as difficult for them."

"Daed, I don't disagree with you. But, I don't understand how that affects my future with Carl."

"What I'm trying to say, daughter, is that you can either look at the fire and its aftermath as the biggest event in your life . . . or you can decide it's just one of many big events you hope to experience. Respect that it happened and come to terms with the reality that it changed you and Carl—and everyone else in the family, too." He lowered his voice. "But then move on."

Walker agreed with their father. "Daed's right. It's time to move on. Maybe past time."

May looked completely confused but nodded.

Chapter 20

Two very long, very awkward days had passed since Ally had returned home. She'd barely seen her father—he seemed to have decided that the only place where he could find solace was in the fields. Each morning, he left early with a picnic lunch in a backpack and stayed out tending his crops for most of the day. Poor Kevin had gone with him the first day, then refused the following morning. It seemed that more complaining than actual work was happening in the fields.

Carl had offered to go with Daed this morning, but Daed had brushed off his offer with lightning speed. Granted, Carl wasn't much of a farmer, but they all knew Daed was ignoring him on principle. He wanted everyone to know that he'd given in to their pressure but he wasn't happy about Ally's upcoming nuptials.

Her mother, on the other hand, seemed to be pretending that the wedding wasn't unexpected and that the only thing that really mattered was what everyone was going to eat. She'd been a busy bee, visiting with neighbors from sunup to sundown, making lists and arranging for different folks to bring dishes, plates, and tablecloths.

But the oddest thing that had happened since her return was the appearance of one of the Schotts' alpacas.

It showed up next to the barn and didn't seemed to be in any hurry to go home again. Glancing at the name on the animal's tag, Ally clicked her tongue against the top of her mouth a few times. "Come on, ah, Dancer. We need to get you home now. Come with me."

Dancer scampered to the left. Just out of her reach.

Remembering that Walker had said many times that alpacas had minds of their own but found comfort in groups, Ally wiggled her fingers and tried to look friendly. "Dancer, I have your best interests at heart. I'll take you back to your silly herd."

If she hadn't known better, Ally could've sworn that Dancer had just given her the evil eye. The alpaca remained exactly where it was. Still as a statue.

Obviously, it was time to make amends. "You're right. Your Santa Claus reindeer herd ain't a bad thing at all. Not silly."

Dancer pawed the ground, making Ally decide that the alpaca's name might have been given to her for good reason. "Please come with me. I'm a friend. Don't be shy."

But Dancer was not falling for her sweet words or coaxing. Not even for a minute.

Now what?

If her parents found out that the alpaca had wandered over, Daed would throw a fit. It didn't seem to matter how many times Carl explained that a bolt of lightning had set the barn on fire and that he didn't hold May responsible for his burns; their father's mind remained unchanged. As far as he was concerned, it was the Schotts' barn that had caused Carl to be hurt, while their daughter had gotten out with only a few burns.

And because Mamm was the way she was, she always took their father's side. Even when she didn't necessarily agree with him.

Ally, Carl, and even Kevin had tried to remind them that forgiveness was a part of their culture. When their words were ignored, Bishop Michael counseled them.

But all her father had done was declare that no one understood the damage that had been done.

Then, of course, the Schotts grew tired of defending themselves and began to resent her parents' blame.

As the years passed—with each one came another operation for Carl—the two families found it easiest to ignore each other completely. Ally and Walker had said that it sometimes felt as if there was an invisible wall separating their two properties. A wall that only the two of them had ever dared to scale.

And perhaps Dancer.

"Dancer, I promise I'm on your side." She grabbed for the alpaca's bridle. "All I want to do is help you. There's nothing wrong or scary about that."

Dancer bared her teeth and screeched.

Just as if Ally had attempted to pull out one of the animal's ridiculously long eyelashes.

Now what? If she left Dancer alone, there was a chance the animal would wander closer to the house. If Daed saw it, he'd flip out—which would be a tragedy for everyone and likely traumatizing for Dancer.

But the stubborn creature wasn't moving.

"What's going on?" Carl asked.

She turned with a huge sigh of relief. "Carl, you are an answer to a prayer. I've never been so happy to see you."

"Thanks. I think." Stepping closer, he looked at the alpaca, who was now staring at him with interest. "What's going on? Did you decide to kidnap an alpaca today?"

"Never. I came up here to check on the feed and found Dancer lying down in the sun."

"Dancer?"

"I read her tag."

His eyebrows rose. "That's a fancy name."

"Didn't you know that they're all named after Santa's reindeer?"

"I did not." He grinned. "How did you find out?"

"Walker."

"Of course." He nodded. "Hmm. Well, how are we going to get Dancer back home?"

"I don't know. I guess I could walk over to the Schotts' house and knock on the door."

"That's quite a distance. I could drive you."

"You could if we trusted Dancer not to wander around our farm in the meantime."

A puzzled look crossed his face. "Ah. Daed."

"Right." Frustrated, she moved closer to the animal. "Dancer, won't you follow me? You need to go home."

Dancer swung her head back toward Carl. And . . . batted her eyelashes?

Carl smiled. "Aren't you a pretty girl?" he cooed. "Dancer, I'm real pleased to make your acquaintance, but I'm pretty sure that Walker and May are wondering where you are. We need to get you home."

"Your speech was adorable. Unfortunately, you're talking to an alpaca, not a young woman."

"Given the way I look, I'm pretty sure Dancer is happier to hear my speech than any woman would be."

"Carl, I promise you don't look that bad."

"I know. Sorry, it was a self-centered comment."

"It's not self-centered, but it does make me sad. I can't change how your skin looks, Carl. I can only tell you the same things Mamm and Daed told you the other night. The scars have faded."

"They have."

"I've always taken them as a sign of how brave and tough you are. You're a survivor, Carl. That's something to be proud of."

He breathed deep. "You're right. I thought I'd come to terms with the way I look, but I seem to be constantly bringing it up. I need to work on that."

"I hope you do. You're going to let life pass you by if you keep looking at your future through a haze of regret."

"I don't regret what I did, Ally. I don't even regret the work the doctors did to help me. It's just that there are times when I ache for the way I used to be."

Just as she was nodding, a voice called out.

"Dancer! Dancer! Where are ya?"

It was Walker. "She's here, Walker! By our feed barn!"

"Don't move!" he called out. "We'll be right there."

We? Ally exchanged a look with Carl. It looked as if they were going to find out how Walker's father treated them when the bishop wasn't present.

There was a copse of trees down a small slope that led to the Schotts' land. Ally heard people tromping through the dried leaves and broken twigs.

Dancer stared at the trees. Her ears moved forward. It was obvious that she was content to wait for whomever was joining them. She didn't seem nervous at all.

"Don't worry, Dancer," she said in her sweetest voice. "Your people will be here soon."

"So much for reminding me that Dancer doesn't know what I'm talking about," Carl murmured.

"Hey, it's not like I'm an alpaca pro either."

Carl grinned before his face slipped into a mask. From out of the trees came Walker and May.

The four of them stared at each other . . . just seconds before Dancer made a happy little noise and trotted right over to Walker.

"Hi, Dancer," he cooed. "You pretty girl. You shouldn't have wandered off. I was worried about you."

The ornery alpaca stepped closer to Walker, obviously anxious for a pet.

Gaping at the two of them, Ally pushed back the burst of jealousy she was feeling. It was a sad day when she was jealous of an alpaca minx.

Chapter 21

There was nothing like a wayward alpaca to act as a reality check. Yes, there was a lot of drama going on between the Schotts and the Hilty family, but regular life continued to go on. Livestock needed to be fed, crops needed to be tended to, and alpacas needed to be given lots of attention or they would get bored and turn to mischief. Which was what Dancer had decided to do.

"I'm really sorry about Dancer wandering over uninvited," May blurted. "I mean, not that she ever would have been invited over to visit."

As Dancer continued to nuzzle Walker as if she'd done nothing more than wander a few feet away from her pen, May steeled herself for Ally's reaction. She wouldn't blame the other woman if she started yelling. After all, Dancer was on her land and had no doubt inconvenienced them.

"I am, too," Ally said. "That blasted Alpaca wouldn't give me the time of day," she joked. "I spoke soothingly and even told her she was pretty. Now, here she is, sidling up to Walker like he's her beau. It's not fair."

"I was starting to think she might eventually like me," Carl said. "Now I realize that she was merely leading me on."

They were actually sounding as if they were jealous of Dancer's attention. It was adorable. "While most alpacas hate being outside their comfort zone or away from their herd, Dancer is the exception. Though she is slow to warm up to people, she actually seems to like everyone," May said. "Her worst trait is that she gets bored. If she feels that she's getting ignored for any period of time, she makes mischief."

"The problem is that Dancer is too smart for her own good," Walker added as he continued to pet Dancer's side. "She taught herself how to open latches on gates and pry open feed boxes, too."

"She's smart and a flirt." Of course, as soon as May heard herself, she wished she could take that back. What kind of proper Amish woman would say such things? Feeling her cheeks heat, she tried to figure out something she could say to ease the awkwardness of the moment.

Carl burst out laughing. "Are you sure you don't have the wrong halter on her? She sounds more like a Vixen."

Stepping away from the animal, Walker shook his head. "*Nee*, Vixen is definitely more vixen-like."

"Just be glad Comet didn't come over," May added. "He's been known to be affectionate—but only until he gets a treat. Then he turns on you."

Walker nodded. "Comet's a heartbreaker, for sure and for certain."

Ally's grin turned even brighter. "I had no idea alpacas had so much personality. Who's your favorite?"

"Donner," Walker said.

"Blitzen is the calmest and most docile."

"So they all have their own personality."

"They sure do, in spades," Walker said. Smiling at Ally, he teased, "Almost like someone I know."

"Do not compare me to an alpaca," Ally said.

"It's a compliment."

"Not to me."

"Are you suggesting that I try harder with my compliments?"

"I am."

"Come with me to take Dancer home. I'll do my best to sing your praises the whole way to the barn."

"What about your family?"

Walker's expression hardened. "I told them I was done with this silly feud." He glanced at Carl. "No offense, Carl, but I canna do anything about the past. I'm sorry you got burned, but that doesn't mean I have to avoid Ally for the rest of my life."

May inhaled sharply. "Walker, you are being rude."

Before Walker could say another word, Carl spoke. "I agree with you completely. Lightning struck an old barn, and it caught on fire. That fire was no one's fault. Not even the Lord's. Lightning strikes the earth." He took a deep breath. "I'm also real tired of being viewed as a victim. I helped May get out of that barn. I made sure she wasn't injured by falling wood or embers. I'm glad I did that."

Ally placed a hand on Carl's shoulder. "Good for you, brother. Now all we have to do is hope our parents will eventually feel the same way."

"That might be wishful thinking, but I truly do think it's possible. One day they are going to have to stop focusing on what they want and unbend enough to see other people's needs."

"Do you feel that's really possible?"

"I do. I mean, I have to."

"And then?"

"And then, I'll look forward to celebrating."

Walker stepped forward. "So you aren't upset about Ally and me seeing each other?"

"I'm surprised, but I don't see why you need my blessing. I've been gone for years, and Ally is a grown woman. She needs my love, not my blessing."

"I'd still like it, though, Carl."

"Then, of course, you have it. I'll do my best to encourage our parents and Kevin to see the light as well."

Walker inclined his head. "*Danke.*"

Carl nodded as well.

Dancer pawed the ground. It was obvious that she wasn't pleased to have lost her position as the focus of the conversation. Walker chuckled. "I think that's my signal to return Dancer to her herd. Ally, would you still like to come with me to the barn?"

"Of course. See ya, Carl."

Opening up the latch on the gate, Walker led Dancer out. "Are you coming, May?"

"I will in a little bit. I'm going to stay here and talk with Carl for a spell."

"Be careful getting home."

"I will."

She smiled up at Carl as Ally closed the gate and walked by Walker's side back toward the Shotts' barn.

"This feud our parents have been perpetuating has gotten out of hand. All of us realize that it is toxic. It sure hasn't done anyone any good to let it continue."

Carl was still gazing at the field on the other side of the fence posts. "I hope you're right. I hope we can all get along one day without Preacher Elias overseeing us all."

"I'm just glad you've returned."

He scanned her face, seeming to be looking for something in her expression. She remained still, gazing at him without hiding her feelings. Trying to let him know that there might be a lot still separating them, but there was still a lot connecting them, too. She was done pretending that she didn't care about him.

Whatever he saw must have shaken him because he reached for her and pulled her close so his hands were loosely clasped around her waist. "I'm not staying here for good, you know."

"I know."

"And I'm not going to change."

She cocked an eyebrow. "Is that right?"

Was she teasing him? Goading him? "I'm not going to be Amish again."

"You've told me that before."

"So . . ."

"So?" She arched an eyebrow. There she was again. Giving him a bit of attitude. He loved that, at first glance, his pretty May seemed like nothing more than a young Amish lady and dutiful daughter. But he'd seen the spark in her eyes from the moment they'd first met all those years ago and had been transfixed. Now that she was all grown up, May seemed to have no problem showing her real personality a lot more often.

The truth was that she was much spunkier than most people realized. That pluck sometimes caught folks off guard— it sure had their teacher in the Amish schoolhouse! But it was May's attitude that had attracted him to her in the first place. It was what had made him follow her around when they were younger and made him still want her now, even though at times she felt like a stranger.

The liveliness of her personality was what drew him like a bee to a pot of honey.

"May, what am I going to do with you?" he muttered, half to himself.

May had heard him, of course. Instead of answering, she just smiled.

It felt like a temptation.

Almost like a dare. That smile warmed his insides, made his mind drift toward things it probably shouldn't dwell on. But at least he had his answer. There really was only one thing he should do with May.

Only one thing that seemed right.

So he kissed her.

Chapter 22

It might be wrong. It might be misguided . . . or maybe even naïve to think that his response meant something. May didn't care. All she knew was that it had been six years since the last time Carl Hilty had kissed her.

No, since anyone had kissed her.

By any accounting, it was far too long.

So instead of acting shy or bashful or maybe even appropriately stunned, May leaned in to Carl's embrace.

With a moan, he wrapped his arms around her and kissed her again.

May felt as if her heart was beating faster, her pulse was racing, and birds were singing. The moment was just that special, and she knew that even if they didn't kiss again for another six years, it was enough to hold inside her heart.

Okay, that was a bit of an exaggeration. She really didn't want to wait another six years for another kiss from Carl. But the moment definitely did feel special.

When he lifted his head, she noticed that his light brown eyes had darkened with emotion and that he seemed to be just as affected as she was.

Then he dropped his hands and stepped back. "Forgive me."

"There's nothing to forgive. I think it's obvious that I wanted to kiss you, too."

Heat sparked in his eyes before he visibly tamped it down. "Oh, my word, May. Even after all this time apart, there is still something between us. I . . . I didn't expect that."

"I felt it, too," she admitted. After all, if he could share such things, then she felt that she could, too.

"Do you ever wonder about the connection between us? Do you ever wonder why the Lord made us next-door neighbors?"

"Not really."

"No? Well, I do." He took a deep breath, seeming anxious about their kiss.

He seemed so full of doubt, she decided to give him a way out. "We're not teenagers anymore, you know. We didn't do anything wrong. At the end of the day, it was just a kiss. Nothing more."

"Hmm."

Now it was her turn to take a deep breath. And let reality return. "Would you please take me home?"

"You're ready?"

No. "It's probably for the best. You know, until we get everything sorted out."

He cast her a sideways look. "You mean Ally and Walker's engagement and marriage taken care of, right?"

She hadn't. She'd been speaking of the two of them. "*Jah.*"

Carl didn't look as if he believed her, but he didn't argue. "Let's get you home, then."

She followed him into the house. After gathering his keys and stuffing his wallet into the back pocket of his chinos, Carl led her to his silver truck.

"Here," he murmured, placing his hands on her waist as he gave her a boost in.

"Thank you."

"Buckle up now."

Again, she did as he asked while he walked around the front of the truck and slid behind the wheel. After turning on the ignition, he pulled onto the street. His right hand was on the wheel, his left arm resting in the space where his window was rolled down. She couldn't help but think that the posture suited him.

"May, you're studying me like I'm a science project. What's wrong?"

"Not a thing. I was, um, just thinking that the truck suits you."

He raised an eyebrow. "More than a buggy?"

She nodded. "I think so. You seem so relaxed, like you were born riding around in trucks all the time. Did you find it easy to take up driving?"

"Easy? No." He stopped at a light. "I didn't get my license until two years ago. It was getting harder and harder for me to ask coworkers to drive me around, and Uber drivers can get expensive. So I haven't been driving very long."

"What was difficult for you?"

"The written test, for one. A lot of the terms simply weren't familiar. It took me two tries to pass it." He smiled at her. "The first time I took the test, I scored around seventy percent. It was humbling, for sure."

"But you studied and got better."

"I did. And I stopped letting my pride get in the way and started asking everyone—even teenagers—about the information in the booklet."

"They helped you?"

"Actually, they helped the most. Most of them still had the test fresh in their minds. They gave me a lot of tips and also helped describe what some things meant in easy-to-understand language. Some of my older friends had been driving for so long they couldn't really describe why they did some things the way they did."

"That makes sense." She was enjoying his story, mainly because it gave her a glimpse into his new life. "So then you took the driver's test?"

"*Nee.* Then I took driver's education class and driving lessons. And had to ask some of my Englisher friends if they'd let me drive them around." He chuckled. "I promise, you never know just how much someone likes you until he or she lets you drive their car. I'm going to owe some people favors for the rest of my life."

She giggled. "I bet you were pretty good."

"All I can say is that I did pass my driving test the first time I took it—but I was a nervous wreck." He pulled into her driveway. "Here you go, May."

She wished they weren't already there. "I wish we'd have more conversations like this," she murmured.

"Like what? You learning about my faults and insecurities?"

"No, us talking about things. I miss just catching up with you and sharing stories. I don't want every conversation to be about our families' problems."

"Or our history."

She nodded, glad that he completely understood. "Those things are important, but they aren't all we are."

"I couldn't agree more. It was the easy conversation we used to share that I've missed the most over the years. With you, I never had to try too hard, May."

Looking into his eyes, she hoped and prayed that they would be able to have lots of these types of talks again. "I'm looking forward to getting to know you again, Carl."

"I want the same thing." He studied her face again, then exhaled. "I'll come around and help you out."

She didn't need his help, but May waited for him to open her door anyway. She took his hand when he reached up to guide her down and leaned close when he pressed his lips to her cheek. "Everything is going to be okay, May," he said. "See you."

"See you." She smiled and gave a little wave as he climbed back in his truck and backed down the drive.

Chapter 23

Aided by the tent in the Shotts' yard, the food truck, and a swarm of people, Ally enjoyed a moment of privacy with her fiancé. "How long do you think we can stay hidden out here before everyone forces us to mingle?"

"Not long."

"What, like an hour?" She was joking, but only a little bit.

"I mean like ten minutes, because we sure aren't hidden, Ally. Everyone can see us. I think all our friends are taking pity on us because this is the worst engagement party in Apple Creek's history."

"I'm pretty sure you're right."

"I know I am." He grimaced. "Our parents will hardly look at each other—and I think there's even something odd going on between Carl and May now."

Ally snorted. "That's not a surprise."

"How come?"

"Come on. You've been living with your sister your whole life, and Carl is the same as he's ever been. Neither of them likes to share how they are really feeling. They're both skilled at keeping things locked up inside."

Walker's eyebrows pulled together. "Ally, what feelings do they have? I thought they were fine with us being together. *Nee*, I know May is glad we're getting married."

"I'm not talking about their feelings for us. I'm talking about their feelings for each other. They're circling around each other like two smitten teenagers who are too bashful to make the first move."

He stared at her, then slowly grinned. "I reckon you have a point there."

"See? That's why we need to stay hidden."

"Ally, darling, I'd do whatever I could for you . . . but it's just not possible. We need to get back into the thick of things so the party won't go from bad to worse." He lifted her knuckles and kissed them. "I promise, years from now, when this is all just a memory, we'll laugh."

She usually hated when people said stuff like that, but he was probably right. "Fine." Then she smiled as he drew her over to Preacher Elias and his wife, Fran.

"Thank you for coming," she said.

"We wouldn't have missed it for the world," Fran said. "Weddings are wonderful, and short engagements all the better, don't you think? So often, people concentrate on all the bells and whistles instead of focusing on marriage and the vows they're about to make."

Thinking of some of the bridal parties she'd been part of, and how every little detail was fussed over, she nodded. "You are probably right. I think *mei mamm* is secretly relieved that this engagement was a sudden one. She's said more than once that she's glad not to have to do too much to get ready for Saturday's wedding."

"I'm sure the meal will be wonderful, and you will be glowing," Fran said with an encouraging smile. "It will be a special day, for sure and for certain."

"I know it will. Thank you both for helping so much."

"It's been our pleasure."

Preacher Elias placed a hand on Walker's shoulder. "And you, Walker? Do you feel ready for the wedding, son?"

Taking Ally's hand again, Walker threaded his fingers through hers. "I do. This event might have been a whirlwind, but my feelings for Ally are true. She's the woman for me, I've no doubt of that. I canna wait until I may call her my wife."

Even though they had an audience, Ally released a happy sigh. "That was so sweet, Walker."

"It's the truth, Ally. I love you."

"You two are simply adorable. A wonderful-*gut* match," Fran said with a smile. "Now Ally . . . pardon the change in topic, but what do you think about the alpacas?"

"Hmm?" The alpacas just happened to be in a nearby pen. The eight of them looked like interested schoolchildren. They were all lined up near the fence, half eating grass and half watching the gathering with interest. One of them even looked a bit put out that she wasn't in the thick of things. "Well, I like alpacas just fine."

Fran giggled. "No, dear. I meant are you going to start helping Walker and May train and show them?"

"*Nee.*"

"What about the wool? Are you going to help your mother-in-law knit caps and such?"

"We haven't talked too much about that."

"I see."

Walker came to the rescue again. "Ally and I haven't had time to discuss everything just yet."

Looking at Ally's midsection, Fran smiled. "Of course, you haven't. Why, I'm sure you both have a great many other things to plan for."

Ally covered her middle with her arms. Carl had said people would assume she was expecting, and he'd been right.

Chapter 24

Amish weddings were long by nature. They usually lasted three hours, with multiple preachers speaking, large amounts of scripture read, lots of prayers, and even more people in attendance. As was their way, the men sat on one side of the aisle, the women on the other. The two groups faced each other, and all tried to listen carefully.

But it was normal for people to get up from time to time, children to walk across the aisle to sit with different parents or with siblings, and worshippers to allow their minds to drift as they waited for the ceremony to reach its inevitable conclusion.

May, sitting in her blue dress next to Ally, did her best to be as attentive and present as she possibly could. After all, it was her brother's wedding day.

However, it was impossible to think only about Walker when Carl was sitting next to him. Every time Preacher Elias asked the bride and groom to stand, her eyes wandered over to Carl. He wasn't dressed Amish, but he certainly blended in more than he usually did. He was wearing a long-sleeved white shirt, dark pants, and a navy vest. As usual, he was clean-shaven, but it looked as if he'd recently trimmed his hair, too.

He was handsome and familiar and yet tantalizingly out of reach. She couldn't seem to look at anyone else.

After they all stood, then sat down again, she glanced back at Carl. This time, he was looking at her. His expression seemed slightly amused, as if he knew that she'd been staring at him far too often during the ceremony. It was mortifying, but what could she do? May shrugged, just to let him know that she couldn't help herself.

He grinned.

She grinned back.

"May, stop flirting with my brother during my wedding ceremony," Ally whispered.

"Sorry, but I can't seem to help it."

"Obviously."

Luckily, a few moments later, Preacher Elias called them to their feet again. Then he beckoned Ally and Walker forward, along with May and Carl. After speaking for another few moments about the sanctity of marriage and the responsibilities of everyone in attendance to help the couple have a long and happy marriage, Elias led Walker and Ally as they recited their vows.

The entire congregation seemed to lean forward as Ally and Walker vowed to love, honor, and cherish each other through good times and bad, through sickness and health.

Ally's voice was clear and filled with joy. Walker's was deep and thick with emotion. Seeing how happy her brother appeared filled May with emotion, too. She glanced at Carl. He seemed equally transfixed. After a second or two, he looked at her directly.

As Elias spoke again, May could see only Carl. Unable to help herself, she remembered the first time he'd talked to her at school. The first time he'd "accidentally" bumped into her and then had laughed when she'd asked if he was blind. The first time he'd announced that he was going to walk her home, practically daring Walker to say a word.

And the moment in that barn when he'd finally, finally pulled her into his arms and she'd put her own hands on his shoulders, thinking that she was the luckiest girl in the world because there was no better boy than Carl Hilty—and he only had eyes for her.

Then, suddenly, Ally and Walker kissed, the crowd cheered, and they were married.

"Congratulations!" she said, giving Ally a hug. "I'm so happy for you both."

"May, we're sisters now!" Ally said.

Her new sister-in-law was glowing. "I know," May said. "It's wonderful-*gut*." She meant it sincerely, too. Ally and Walker had helped mend the rift between their families. Their love and marriage were irreversible, and everyone in attendance would help all four parents to see that their feud could not go on forever. It was no longer a possibility.

As Ally was hugged by Kevin, May reached for her brother. "Congratulations!" She was all smiles as she rose on her tip-toes and kissed him on the cheek.

Walker held her close. He owed May a lot. If she hadn't given him and Ally so much support, he would probably still be sneaking around the Holsts' property waiting to meet Ally in the middle of the night. "*Danke*, May. I am very happy."

"You look happy, too," she said. "Walker, I am thrilled for you, and I think God is, too. I know this wedding was the right thing to happen. You and Ally deserve to be to-gether. I wish you many, many happy years together."

"*Danke*," he said again. Then he lowered his voice. "Now

all we have to do is wait for you and Carl to do the same thing."

Her emotions danced a little jig before reality returned. Because even if she wanted to have the same kind of traditional Amish wedding as her brother, it was impossible. Carl was English now.

She didn't fault him for that.

She just didn't know what it meant for her.

Chapter 25

Carl hadn't been to an Amish wedding in years. Not since he was a teenager, hanging out with Ally and Kevin in the background, half bored, trying to snag a couple of cookies and extra plates of food without being told to stay out of the way.

Now, seeing the union from an adult's perspective, he had to admit that the whole afternoon had been a beautiful affair. The words of the preacher meant something—and not just because the vows that were spoken were the same ones that generations of their families had said before them. The pure love that was so evident between his sister and Walker had been wonderful to see. He'd never thought of himself as the romantic type, but witnessing them exchanging vows had gotten him choked up. He was happy that his sister was safe and content. Now she would always have Walker Schott looking after her and making sure she didn't feel alone in the world.

Which, he realized, said a lot about his feelings. He'd never wanted to admit it, but he'd felt all alone in the world many times over the last couple of years. Not only had he been in pain, but he'd had to learn to fit in, educate himself about so many things that all his coworkers took for granted . . . and, of course, learn to live with his scars.

And live without May.

"Hiya, Carl."

The pretty feminine voice made him turn around. The face looking up at him wasn't the one he'd expected to see. Instead of May's warm brown eyes and adorably full cheeks, it was someone else entirely. "Felicity, *jah?*"

"*Jah.*" Felicity's light blue eyes looked confused. "You really don't recognize me?"

"I thought it was, but we haven't seen each other in years, you know."

"We saw each other at your welcome home party. You smiled at me then and said it was good to see me."

"It was." He was frustrated with himself and with her. What in the world did she want him to say? "How are you? The wedding was lovely, didn't you think?"

"I did. I was surprised that Walker and Ally had such a short engagement, but I guess it couldn't be helped, right?" She winked.

"What are you referring to?"

She smiled. "Come on, Carl. You and I are old enough that we don't need to pretend. No one's shocked."

"You obviously are, since you brought it up."

All traces of humor vanished from her expression. "I didn't mean anything, Carl. I'm just making conversation."

"About my sister. Or have you forgotten that?"

"*Nee.* Of course not." She looked pained. "I'm sorry if I offended you."

"You did. If I hear more rumors circulating about why Ally and Walker got married, I'm going to place the blame firmly on you."

"All I did was share what I've heard."

"It was in very poor taste."

"You've . . . you've gotten so . . . so—"

"What?"

Felicity opened her mouth, then turned away before uttering another word. He was grateful for that small favor.

"I see you're enjoying yourself, Carl," May said as she wrapped a hand around his elbow. "Come take a walk with me."

"May, I don't want to walk."

"I'm afraid it's very necessary right now. You need a break, and Felicity needs to salvage some of her pride." May tugged on his arm again. "Come on, Carl."

"Fine." He adjusted her grip on his arm so it looked as if he was escorting her instead of being led around like a recalcitrant child. "How much of our exchange did you overhear?"

"Only the part about how Felicity had been talking about your sister and that if you heard further rumors you were going to blame her." Her lips twitched.

"I guess that was laying it on a bit thick."

"Only a little bit." She peeked up at him. "Felicity deserved it, though. I don't know what she was thinking, saying something like that, bold as brass."

"Right?" After making sure they were out of earshot of everyone else, he added, "It was almost like she assumed I'd come right out and say that *mei* sister had . . . had . . ."

"Anticipated her wedding night?" she murmured.

He laughed. "Well, that's one way of saying it." Thinking of how upset the girl had looked, Carl winced. "I hope Felicity doesn't go about sharing how rude I was."

"She wouldn't dare. I gave her a hard look when she was acting all upset. She suddenly started acting a lot more circumspect."

"And then you came over and helped me, too."

"I'm a really good friend to you, Carl."

"Yes, you are. *Danke.*" When May chuckled again, he couldn't help but smile. "You're in a good mood. You're happy, aren't you?"

"I am. Walker is so in love. He was willing to do anything in order to marry Ally. And Ally felt the same way. Even though they are our siblings, I think seeing a couple like that, so determined to be together . . . it makes a person believe in love again, you know?"

"I know." He dropped his arm and reached for both of her hands, linking their fingers. "No matter what happens between our families, you and I will always have this day to celebrate. We did a good thing when we went to them and offered our support."

She nodded. "I guess we did do that."

He wasn't sure, but it seemed that May's smile dimmed a bit as she dropped her hands. "Well, I suppose I'd better get back." As a cheer rang out, her eyes widened. "Oh, it looks like everyone is getting into the buffet lines. We'd better rejoin the wedding party. Ally and Walker are going to wonder what happened to us."

"You're right." He was about to offer his arm again, but May had already started forward. He slowed his pace . . . allowing her to go forward.

He needed another moment to gather himself together anyway.

Chapter 26

It was becoming something of a joke around the house that it might have taken a feud, a torrent of tears, and a whole lot of prayers to get Walker and Ally married, but it had taken absolutely no effort to get used to having Ally there. She fit into their family seamlessly. So much so, it often felt as if May's mother had always relied on Ally to help with the laundry and that Walker had always lived in the *dawdi haus* and breakfasted there.

The only bad part about the new arrangement was that Ally's parents still couldn't seem to move on. They acted as if Ally had left them out of spite. Even though Ally still walked over to help her mother, she wouldn't allow Walker or even May to come over as well. May felt awful about that. She would've been glad to help Ally clean her parents' house or at least do laundry. Ally, at least, seemed to take their attitude in stride, saying that she could put up with a lot because she and Walker were married.

May had been thinking about Ally all day, ever since Walker had relayed that his bride had walked over to her parents' house right after breakfast. The weather was strange that afternoon. The clouds were dark; there was a hint of rain in the air, but there was also an earie stillness. The hens had been clucking and ornery that morning, the horses seemed skittish, and even the usual array of birds that congregated around the feeder seemed to have disappeared.

In addition, all of the alpacas had been acting skittish, frightened of their own shadows.

When the lot of them barely ate their food, her father had guided them outside to their two separate pens, males in one and females in the other. Unfortunately, none of the eight animals looked all that pleased to be out of the barn.

"What is going on with them, Daed?"

"I couldn't say." He rested his hands on the top rail and watched them wander around restlessly. "I've never seen any of them like this."

"I hope they aren't sick."

"I hope not, too, but I'd surprised if they are." He shrugged. "Maybe they're just all in a bad mood today. I reckon everyone's entitled to that—even our furry friends."

She smiled at him, but May wasn't sure that was all that was wrong. A few of the alpacas, such as Blitzen, got easily spooked but others, like Prancer, were usually even-keeled. Prancer was generally the happiest of alpacas. Today he was pawing the ground.

After they finished cleaning the stalls, her father hitched up the buggy and went over to one of their neighbor's. "Ryan's heifer is due any day. I'm gonna go see how she's faring."

"All right." May had a feeling he was simply annoyed with the animals' restless spirit.

She was in the females' pen when Carl's now-familiar gray truck pulled up.

"Hiya, May!" he called out as Walker exited the vehicle.

Happy to see Carl, she said, "Are you staying for a while?"

"I wish I could, but I can't. I have to go do some work. I'll try to see you later."

She waved as he backed out. She understood but was disappointed. After the wedding, Carl had started spending half the week in Cleveland. They hardly saw each other anymore, sometimes only for a few hours a week.

Watching the vehicle leave, May sighed. When were things ever going to get easier? It seemed all they ever did was compare schedules or simply wave to each other from a distance.

Shaking off her thoughts, she smiled at her brother, who had come to stand on the other side of the fence. "*Gut* afternoon. Did you go to the feed store?"

"*Jah*. I ordered more feed, supplements, and some fresh straw. They said they'd drop off the order tomorrow, so Carl and I didn't have to try to load it all into his truck."

"That's a blessing."

"For sure it was. Carl was pleased, especially. His phone was dinging and ringing nonstop." Gazing at the alpacas, he frowned. "How are things around here?"

"Odd. All the animals are acting strange, especially the alpacas. Daed and I thought maybe they'd enjoy some fresh air, but it didn't seem to do much good."

"A big storm is coming. Carl was headed back to his house to make sure his parents and Ally are getting prepared. Is that what Daed is doing?"

"He went over to Ryan Lipscomb's farm to see their heifer."

"I don't think she's birthed that calf yet."

She chuckled. "I think he was more eager to get out of here than worried about the cow. You know how Daed gets when the alpacas act fussy."

"*Jah*. His patience vanishes like a firefly in the fall."

She shrugged. "It was fine with me. We all know these critters aren't real fond of being told what to do."

"I wish he'd stayed around here. Did he take the buggy?"

"He did."

"Okay, so Daisy is with him."

"*Jah*. She is a very reliable mare. Hey, Walker, you really are worried about the weather, aren't you?"

"I am."

She looked up at the sky. "The clouds look a little darker, don't they? It's just rain, though."

He shook his head. "No, there's something else going on. The sky looks really ominous." Still frowning, he added, "Randy over at the feed store told me that he heard the weather forecasters are telling everyone to get their storm cellars prepped."

"For what?"

"Tornadoes. The county is under a tornado watch."

A shiver ran through her, but she firmly brushed it off. "Daed says weathermen like to make big deals out of nothing so people will run to the stores."

Walker rolled his eyes. "May, when are you going to stop thinking that everything our father says is right?"

"I've never said that."

"You don't need to."

"I don't remember us ever having a real tornado in the county, do you?"

"I'm not sure when the last one was, but that doesn't matter. What matters is there's a pretty good chance of one happening today. We need to get the alpacas back inside the barn."

Taking a peek at the two groups, May figured that wouldn't be a bad idea. Alpacas were notorious for being afraid of practically everything. They were especially frightened of thunder and lightning. She couldn't even imagine how they were going to react if a tornado did touch down nearby. "I'll start bringing them in. Will you go tell Mamm what's happening?"

"Sure." Just as Walker peered up at the sky again, rain started to fall.

One of the alpacas made a high-pitched cry. Boy, they hated to get wet.

"I'm coming to save you from the rain!" May called out.

Blitzen's ears popped up, and he trotted directly toward the gate. The other alpacas, happy to follow his lead, gathered around the gate as well.

May could practically feel all eight sets of dark eyes watching her intently—and with impatience. She opened up the males' gate first and guided the three males back into the barn. They went docilely because Blitzen was leading them.

After closing their section of the barn, she hurried to the females' side. Unfortunately, they had gotten themselves into a tizzy. Dancer, usually the head female alpaca, was particularly perturbed. She pawed at the ground. Dasher and Cupid tried to push her aside.

Knowing that yelling would only make them more upset, May did her best to lead Dancer to the barn. The alpaca cried and tried to fight May's lead, but at last she was inside. The others were easier to manage but still took some time to relocate.

Now that they were secure in the barn and rain was no longer pelting them, all eight acted calmer.

She turned on the hose and gave them all plenty of fresh water.

The barn door opened. "May, are they good?"

"I think so. I'm just getting them watered."

"Mamm and I just went to the storm cellar and opened the door. Come on. We need to take some water and food down there."

"Daed isn't even home. Don't you think you're over-reacting?"

"*Nee.* If the storm gets worse, Daed's going to have to keep Daisy in his friend's barn. We need to be prepared."

"But what about the alpacas? Someone is going to have to stay with them."

"No way. We need to get to the cellar."

The cellar was the last place she wanted to go. Not only did she hate being confined in the dark, but there were bugs and critters down there. "I think I'll stay up here. You know what, I'll just go in the barn. Someone ought to keep an eye on the animals, you know."

"*Nee*, May. It's too dangerous. This barn isn't solid enough to survive a strong tornado." His voice had deepened. "Listen, I know this is hard, but we can't pretend it's not happening. Tornadoes have hit in the area before. You know that."

Knowing he was right, she bit back the last of her arguments and hurried to the house. She found her mother scurrying around the kitchen as if her feet were on fire. "Mamm, Walker's here and opening the cellar. What do you need help with?"

"What about your father?"

"He took the buggy to the Lipscombs'. He seemed to think one of their cows was in labor or something."

"That stubborn man. And Ally?"

"Ally is still with her parents. And Carl is going to be over there, too."

Concern filled her eyes as she stared out at the sheets of rain that were now falling from the sky. "I wish Ally was back home with her husband, but I suppose it can't be helped."

May reached out and clasped her hand. "Mamm, all we can do is take care of ourselves now, *jah*?" Her mother didn't respond at first, but then she nodded. Relieved, May asked gently, "What should I do?"

"Fill ten mason jars with water and carry them into the cellar. By the time you finish that, I should have food and blankets ready."

Though May still felt they should be either trying to get hold of their father or doing more for the alpacas, she did as her mother asked. One after the other, she filled the glass jars, tightening the metal caps securely. She put six in a sturdy straw basket and carried them to the cellar, then slowly descended.

Walker had turned on two battery-operated lanterns. Their faint yellow glow welcomed her, but the darkness still felt oppressive. Even before the fire, she'd always been a little afraid to sit in the cellar for very long. Her imagination would get the better of her, and she would start wondering if she was going to be trapped inside.

"May, I decided to open the pens in the barn," Walker said as he joined her.

"Are you sure about that?"

He nodded. "If the winds get bad and a window pane breaks or part of the roof blows off, I want the alpacas to be able to move around at least a little bit."

"I guess that's for the best. It's not like we're going to have any idea what's happening if we're stuck in the cellar."

"Exactly."

She hurried up to get more jars, and then grabbed the tins of cookies and trail mix her mother had put out. "Is this it, Mamm?"

"*Nee*. I'm gathering blankets. Take those jars and then come back."

Again and again, she went back and forth, gathering extra blankets, more flashlights, and books. Walker ended up shuttling their mother out of the house when it was obvious that she intended to put half of their belongings in the cellar. All the while, the rain got heavier, and the winds grew stronger.

By the time she, Walker, and her mother were secure in the cellar, there was a faint glow in the sky. The air was thick and seemed unnaturally still.

Something bad was about to happen. It was obvious that all of them—from the hens to the livestock to the three humans nestled in the tight, dark confines of the storm cellar—were aware of it. Everyone was hunkered down, waiting for the inevitable to occur.

May, sitting on a folding camp chair, took off her shoes, placed her feet on the seat of the chair, and curved her arms around her legs.

"I wish your father hadn't left," Mamm said. "I wish he was down here with us."

"I know you do, Mamm," Walker murmured. "I feel the same way about Ally."

"They'll be all right," May said after a few more moments passed.

"Yes. Of course," Mamm murmured just as the wind picked up speed again.

Walker stared at the cellar door and grimaced. "This is gonna be bad."

May didn't say a word, but she figured he was right. All they could do now was sit and wait and pray.

Chapter 27

After dropping off Walker, Carl drove to the Dollar Store and stocked up on batteries, water bottles, snacks, and instant coffee. He was just pulling out of the parking lot and headed for home when a siren from the emergency broadcast system blared out of the radio.

He turned up the radio as he pushed down on the accelerator. A voice called for attention, announcing severe weather and a tornado watch for their county.

As the rain began to fall harder and the wind picked up, Carl put both of his hands on the steering wheel. His truck's wheels were starting to slide a bit.

When the announcement turned even more urgent, advising everyone to take cover, he wished he hadn't taken the detour to the Dollar Store but had gone right home instead.

The voice on the radio continued, informing them all that funnel clouds had been spotted in their county. The tornado watch had moved into a warning.

"Please be advised to take cover immediately," the voice intoned, leaving no room for argument.

Giving thanks once again that he'd decided to come back to Apple Creek, he parked next to his parents' house and hurried inside. As he'd expected, they were blissfully unaware of how bad the storm actually was.

Ally was rolling out a piecrust, their mother was stirring something at the stove, Kevin was cleaning some tools in the mud room's stationary tub, and their father was sitting in the living room reading the paper.

"Hiya, Carl," Kevin said. "Where've you been?"

"I dropped off Walker, then ran to the Dollar Store."

"What did you get?" Ally asked.

"Things to hold us over for a bit. We need to get to the basement."

No one moved—or even acted as if they'd heard him.

"Hi, Carl. Be sure to take off your boots," Mamm said. "I mopped the floor this morning."

He dutifully toed off his boots and set them in the shoe tray. "They're off, but we all need to go down to the basement now." When no one moved, he raised his voice. "I'm serious. Let's go."

Kevin turned off the faucet. "How come we've got to go down there?"

"I just heard a radio report in my truck. The tornado watch has been upgraded to a tornado warning."

"A warning?" Ally asked.

"That means they saw one in the county. Come on now. We're in danger."

They all stared at him, then as if the Lord had figured Carl needed some help, a fierce crack of thunder boomed overhead. All of them jumped.

Their father sprang into action. "You all heard Carl. Let's get going. Everyone get what you need and be in the basement in two minutes. Sooner if you can. Robin, don't forget to turn off the oven."

Ally quickly rolled the piecrust into the waxed paper she had nearby and popped it into the refrigerator. Carl went upstairs to his room and got his laptop. Thinking that it was better to be safe than sorry, he grabbed a coat, and a blanket and pillow, too. When he walked into the hall, he saw that Kevin had done the same thing.

"You too?" he joked.

Kevin nodded. "A guy at school told me that he hadn't thought about all his clothes and bedding being gone when he had to evacuate for a fire last summer. It made me think that it's better to be safe than sorry."

"That's smart."

When they saw Ally still in the kitchen, Carl called out to her. "Do you still have any of your stuff here? Old clothes? Go get your things now."

"They'll be fine."

"They won't if it's as bad as they're saying. Hurry, now."

Thankfully, Ally hurried up the stairs just as their father called out for Kevin.

"We need to see to the animals, boy."

"*Jah*, Daed." Turning to Carl, he thrust his belongings into his arms. "Put that downstairs, wouldya?"

"*Jah*, but hurry."

"We canna neglect the animals, Carl. Ain't so?"

"I know, but hurry."

"We will. Rest easy, now."

As much as Carl wished everyone was already in the basement, he held his tongue and simply helped his mother check for water and flashlights.

"Here's four, but I'm not sure if we have enough batteries."

"I brought batteries. Let's go down to the basement."

"You get Ally. I'm going to grab some cookies I made."

"Mamm."

"We've been through this before, son," she said gently. "I know what needs to be done."

When the thunder crashed again, the hair on his arms stood on end. This was no regular thunderstorm. Not by a long shot. As his mother disappeared back into the kitchen, he called upstairs for Ally.

"What's taking you so long?"

She appeared on the landing. Tears were in her eyes. "I wish I was home."

"With Walker."

"Of course, with him. He's my home now."

Meeting her at the foot of the stairs, he wiped a stray tear from her face and kissed her brow. "I understand, but there's nothing you can do. I dropped Walker off. He's likely doing the same thing that I am."

"Yelling at family members?"

"Herding cats. Come on."

"What about Mamm?"

"Ally Schott, do you really want me to tell your new husband that you wouldn't head down to the basement to avoid a tornado?"

"I'm going."

He raised his voice. "Come on, Mamm. Let me help you."

At last, she popped out with a tray filled with cookies and two boxes of crackers under an arm. "I'm ready now."

"Ally's downstairs." Lowering his voice, he added, "She's teary-eyed because she's away from Walker."

"Uh oh. Is your father down there?"

"*Nee.*"

"I better go talk to her before your father gets downstairs."

"Good idea." When she headed down, Carl breathed a sigh of relief. "Two."

Just as another bolt of lightning hit, the back door opened, and Kevin and their father strode in. Both were wet.

"Mamm and Ally are in the basement."

"What are you waiting for, son? Come on. Let's get down there."

Shaking his head, Carl followed the other two. When they were sitting in the small room with the low ceiling and cement floor, he breathed a sigh of relief. At least all five of them were safe.

Less than two minutes later, four of the five of them were camped out on the two old couches that had belonged to his grandparents. The basement had narrow windows lining the top of the walls. Usually they let in natural light, but the skies had darkened, and rain pelted them. Kevin, wrapped in a blanket, was standing on a step stool and peering out. "I think it's getting worse!"

"Maybe I should've left the barn door open," Daed fretted. "If something does happen, the animals will need to get out. Maybe I should—"

"*Nee,*" Carl, Ally, and Kevin said at the same time.

"I can't worry about you being out there," Mamm announced.

"But what about Buttercup?"

"I love that horse, but I love you more. Stay."

"There's a glow in the sky, and the wind is real fierce now," Kevin called out. "Oh! I think the barn door just blew open."

"Now they'll be able to get out if they need to," Carl said.

Daed pursed his lips. "Maybe."

"I hope the chickens will be okay," Ally said.

"Me, too," Mamm said. "They're likely squawking up a storm."

When another burst of wind crashed against the house, causing the windowpanes to rattle, Ally reached for Carl's hand. "I'm worried about Walker and May," she whispered. "I wish I was there."

"I know. Walker will be glad you're safe, though." Thinking about May, he murmured, "I keep thinking about May. She really hates the dark. Do they have a basement?"

"*Nee*. Only a storm cellar. Walker told me about it the other day. Just in passing, though. He didn't take me down there. He said it was unpleasant in the best of situations."

"I reckon that's where they'll be now."

She shivered. "Walker said that May is afraid to go down there."

"She's afraid of the dark." After glancing at their parents, he added, "May told me that ever since the fire, she doesn't like being in small spaces or in the dark."

"She's going to hate being down there."

"*Jah*." He rubbed the back of his neck. He hated the thought of her being not only afraid of the tornado but also pummeled with memories of the fire. "I hope her family will be understanding with her."

"I'm sure they will be. The Schotts are good people." Lowering her voice, she murmured, "I know you have feelings for May, Carl. Don't you think it's time you did something about them?"

Yes. Yes, he did. "May and I will be okay," he said instead. "We always are."

"It's hailing!" Kevin called out.

"Come sit down, child," Mamm called. "Now, does anyone want a sandwich?"

"We've been down here twenty minutes, Robin," Daed chided. "We're fine."

Even though there were so many things to worry about, the words made Carl grin. Some things never did change.

Chapter 28

May used to wake up screaming in the middle of the night. Almost every evening, she'd dream of the same scene. She would lure an unsuspecting Carl into the barn, then the sky would suddenly get dark. Following that would be the clap of thunder and the strike of lightning that set the barn afire.

Usually, then, the barn doors would be shut fast, the flames would be spreading, and she'd watch Carl's clothes catch on fire.

It was a horrible dream, petrifying and chaotic, with a good dose of guilt and angst thrown in. It had been so bad that she'd begun to try not to sleep just so she wouldn't have to experience it all over again. Of course, eventually exhaustion would take over. She soon became short-tempered and forgetful. Shadows formed under her eyes, and tears flowed at even the smallest upset.

After this continued for several weeks, her mother had taken her to first the bishop, then a nurse, then finally an English therapist, who suggested that May should keep a flashlight on at night and even keep a window cracked open.

Both served to remind her that she was in a snug bed instead of back in that burning barn.

Little by little, her night terrors eased. Within six months, she no longer had to have the window open. Then she only had to have the dimmest of lights shining. Soon, the only reminders of her trauma were the fierce feeling of guilt she felt about her actions that night and the weight of Carl's absence from her life. She'd missed him so much.

May hadn't had a nightmare in months. Though she still wasn't comfortable in dark places or near fires, May felt she had recovered.

Until about ten minutes ago. Now she was pretty sure that every single one of her fears had returned, in full force.

May hadn't thought she had any reoccurring issues from the fire, but after spending thirty minutes in the storm cellar, she realized that being in an enclosed, dark space still terrified her. Even though the circumstances were far different, she still felt trapped. As each minute passed, her skin felt more clammy, and her heart rate quickened. It was awful to realize that all her insecurities could return so quickly.

May began to pray for peace—and to stare at the closed door above their heads as if it were a hateful enemy.

"I wish there was a window in here," she whispered, mainly to herself.

"If we had a window, it wouldn't be much of a storm cellar, would it?" Walker joked.

"*Nee*, but it would sure make me feel better."

"Try not to think about it, May," Mamm cautioned. "Stewing on negative things will only make you feel worse."

That was easier said than done, especially since they were currently huddled in their basement hoping a tornado wasn't going to hit their house.

"Hey," Walker said in a low tone, "I think Mamm is right. Let's both try to be thankful for our blessings instead of our worries right now."

"Is that working for you?" She knew she was being sarcastic, but she didn't enjoy having her mother treat her like a child—or assuming that her issues were easily solved.

Looking bemused, he shook his head. "Nope. All I can think about is that my wife is on another farm when I should be the one taking care of her."

Noticing that their mother was knitting, May said, "Do you really feel that way? I mean, you two just got married."

"I do. I can't help it, either. It's as if the moment the Lord encouraged us to say our vows, Ally became mine." His eyes lit up. "I don't want to start ordering her around or anything, but I do want to care for her. I promised myself that she wouldn't ever have to feel as if she doesn't have someone on her side. I like having that responsibility."

"That's so sweet."

He leaned closer. "You know you and Carl are going to be that way, too."

"I don't know. Things between us aren't the same. Carl has a far different life in Cleveland. He's happy there, too."

"Does that mean you wouldn't be, too?"

May was shocked by his question. "Are you saying that you think I should follow in his footsteps?"

"No, but I am saying that if you are expecting everything in our lives to be suddenly organized and happy, I think you're going to be waiting a long time."

"Given that we're seeking shelter in a storm cellar because a tornado was spotted nearby, you might be right."

He laughed. "I guess if I needed a sign from the Lord, I just found one, didn't I? But seriously, all I'm saying is that I have a feeling that if the two of you open your hearts, you're gonna find a place where you both fit in."

"I don't know where that place might be. We have to live in either Apple Creek or Cleveland."

"*Nee*, May. I'm not talking about specific towns. I'm talking about a state of being. You two need to decide how you want to live your lives together. Once you do that, everything else will fall into place."

She raised her eyebrows. "Who knew you could be so poetic—or make so much sense?"

"Ally, for one." His grin made her chuckle. "Why do you think I married her?"

"Bingo." She held up a hand and fist-bumped him.

"It sure is nice to see the two of you getting along so well," Mamm murmured.

"We always get along," Walker said.

"Hmm."

May shared a smile with her brother. Then, realizing that the wind had died down, she glanced at her mother, who was still knitting next to a battery-powered lantern. "Mamm, I think the weather has cleared. Can I peek outside?"

"Of course not. We're under a tornado warning, remember?"

"The wind sounds calmer. Maybe the storm has passed."

Of course, just then, the wind picked up, and a loud clap of thunder reverberated in the air.

"I don't think the storm has passed yet," Mamm said in a mastery of understatement.

May slumped against the wall. "I guess not."

"Try to relax, sister," Walker urged. "We're safe."

"I'm trying."

When Walker picked up a book, and her mother returned to her knitting, May closed her eyes and tried to pray. *Dear Father, who art in heaven. Hallowed be thy name.*

But even the simple, well-known Lord's Prayer seemed to be too much. Her thoughts kept skipping around like stones in a churning river. Releasing a ragged sigh, she stared at the door again.

Her mother put down her book. "May, what is wrong? I've never seen you act so afraid of thunder and lightning."

"It's not the storm that's bothering me. It's being stuck here in the dark."

"I don't understand."

"I feel like I'm back in the barn."

"This reminds you of the fire?"

She nodded. "*Jah*. I . . . I feel trapped, like I did when I was in that barn and didn't know how I was going to get out."

Walker narrowed his eyes. "I didn't know you felt trapped."

Now all three members of her family were staring at her with various degrees of confusion and concern. She shifted uneasily. Had they forgotten what had happened . . . or had she never told them the whole truth about her actions?

"When the lightning struck the barn and it caught fire, Carl and I were in the back corner. Where we groom the alpacas now. The wood caught so fast, one whole wall practically burst into flames seconds after the lightning bolt hit. We had to pass by it in order to get out."

Her mother nodded. "*Jah*, you told us that."

"And Carl encouraged you to get out."

"What I never told you was that I couldn't move. My feet felt frozen. I was paralyzed by fear. Carl kept trying to get me to move . . . no, begging me to move." She swallowed, sharing her greatest guilt. "I fought him."

"I think you're being too hard on yourself," Mamm said. "I'm sure you weren't being difficult. Besides, you were young."

"Not too young to know better."

"Come on, May. That barn was on fire," Walker pointed out. "It looked like it was about to explode any minute. I was pretty sure I'd just lost you forever."

As much as she appreciated her family's efforts to make her feel better, she couldn't let them continue. "It was a bad situation—I'm not going to deny that. But I didn't react well. I practically fought Carl. He kept tugging on my hand, but I was screaming and crying . . . and every second that passed, the flames got bigger and bigger."

Remembering how smoky it was and the scent of the burning wood, May shivered. "Carl ended up having to wrap his arms around my body and half-carry me. He shielded my body to get us out." Filled with shame, she added, "It's all my fault Carl got such terrible burns. If I hadn't been so scared or afraid, Carl would've been okay."

Her mother swallowed. "May, I'm sure you're remembering things differently from how it was."

"I'm not. Haven't you ever wondered why Carl's left side is so much more damaged than his right? How we got out at the same time but I only had a few burns, while Carl's injuries were so awful that he had to get life-flighted out to a burn unit? It's because he shielded me."

She swiped away one of the tears that were sliding down her cheeks. "Carl saved my life six years ago. And for his trouble, he not only had to endure weeks and months of painful surgeries and treatments, but he had to leave his home. Now he doesn't even feel comfortable being in Apple Creek—or Amish. It is all my fault."

"Neither Able nor Robin ever said a word about that. All either of them told us was that Carl was brave and saved you."

Walker glared. "I can't believe you never told us the full story. You should have."

"I know. I tried. I wanted to. It's just that, at first, I was shaken up; then I was so worried about Carl. And then I didn't know how to correct your version of what had happened."

"It wouldn't have been that hard," Walker retorted. "All you had to do was simply tell us the truth. You let your pride rule your mouth."

She hung her head. "You're right. That's exactly what I did."

"I wish you'd told us, May," Mamm said. "If you had, I would've been more understanding about Able and Robin's anger."

"I am sorry."

Walker stood up. "If our families had gotten along better, Ally and I might not have had to sneak around all this time."

"I am willing to take responsibility for my weakness. Of course, I've apologized to Carl many times. He knows I feel terrible about my actions. Also, I didn't do any of it on purpose. I was literally petrified. Since I don't think any of you have been trapped in a burning barn before, you can't say how you would react if you had been in my shoes."

"Maybe not, but I wouldn't have simply stood there," Walker said. "I also sure wouldn't have talked for years like my actions were better than they were."

May knew she was at fault, but she wasn't willing to be put down for being human. "Am I the only one who has let pride stand in the way of what is right? Walker, couldn't you and Ally have simply stood up to both sets of parents together? You two are adults, not children."

"Daughter, it is not your place to say so."

"All right. But also, Mamm and Daed, you remind me all the time to forgive and to be honest. But couldn't you have tried harder to reach out to Able and Robin? You used to be really close to them. It's been six years, after all.

"Fine." She crossed her arms and went back to staring at the closed cellar door. Then flinched as hail began to fall.

Mamm gasped. "Oh, no. The storm has gotten worse."

There was a rumble that sounded like a train was charging through their land, and May pressed one hand against the wall.

The wind picked up; then hail fell even harder. It sounded as if each pellet was a hammer hitting the storm cellar door.

Then it felt as if all the air was being pulled out of the cracks between the door and the cellar walls.

"It's coming," Mamm called out. "Pray!"

With the roar of a locomotive tearing through their front yard, the tornado hit, and May closed her eyes.

Once again, her mind went blank, and her muscles froze. Once again, as panic gripped her, May couldn't think, couldn't move. She couldn't seem to do anything but tremble as the noise got even louder, and everything shook.

It was obvious that debris and tree limbs were hitting the storm-shelter door. Her imagination took over. She pictured the whole house flying into pieces. All her belongings—her only home—disappearing into a stack of sticks and rubble.

She took a deep breath, reminding herself that such things didn't matter. Her father was likely with the Lipscombs, and the three of them were safe.

And then she remembered the animals. Jack and Jill, their two plow horses, the cow, the chickens, and all the alpacas. "Our poor animals!"

"I know," Mamm said weakly. "But there's nothing we can do but wait."

Wait and pray. At last, feeling as if everything was lost, she closed her eyes and prayed for Carl and his family and for their animals and for their house.

But most of all, she prayed for the strength to survive whatever came next.

Chapter 29

Carl was sure no storm had ever lasted so long. As the wind continued to howl, and rain continued to pelt the narrow windows that lined the top of their basement, he watched the other four members of his family lounge on the old living room furniture. They all looked comfortable and somewhat bored.

He felt the complete opposite.

Unable to sit still, Carl paced the length of the room. Though he often felt a bit like a fish out of water these days, it was moments like this when he felt it the most. The truth was that he'd been gone from Apple Creek a long time, and neither he, nor his family, nor even the house were the same as when he'd left it.

During the six years that he'd been gone, his family's finances had taken a turn for the better. His father had not only gotten a good price for his corn and alfalfa, but they'd also leased part of their land to a family new to the area. The young couple paid his parents rent every month.

In addition, his mother's quilting expertise had become

widely known. Customers had shown off their quilts and told others about Robin Hilty's impressive craftsmanship. She was now selling ten quilts a year, each one for an impressive amount of money. Mamm had eventually decided to buy new living room furniture with a portion of her proceeds.

In addition, his father had put in a fireplace in the basement, and Kevin had helped him paint the floor with epoxy. They'd also put in a propane-powered light, giving the space a warm glow.

Carl had been shocked the first time he'd seen the basement. It was comfortable and attractive—the polar opposite of the cold, damp space where he and Ally used to play hide and seek when they were small.

"Want to play a game with us, Carl?" Ally asked. "We're going to play cards."

"*Danke*, but no."

"Come on, please? It's better than staring out those tiny windows and worrying."

"Ally's right," Kevin said. "Don't forget that we get tornado watches at least once a year. Sometimes a whole lot more than that."

Sometimes his sixteen-year-old brother sounded wise beyond his years. He really had stepped up in Carl's absence and become a huge help to the family. "I hear what you're saying. I'm not ready to sit down, though. Sorry."

His mother, who was piecing together fabric for one of her quilts, gazed at him sympathetically. "I bet this silence is jarring for you. You're used to being in the city around all your electronics."

"I am." He didn't think that was the cause of his unease, but it felt like a good enough excuse. "I'll relax in a bit. Don't worry about me."

"It's hard to ignore ya, what with you looking so pensive,

boy," Daed said. "The house is secure. Don't forget that we've got a sturdy metal barn, too. It ain't going nowhere."

"What about the Schotts' *haus*?"

"What about it?" His father's voice was frigid.

"Do they have a metal-framed barn now, too?"

Daed shrugged. "How would I know? We barely talk, you know."

"They don't," Ally said. "The barn is wooden, just like the old one."

"How come they didn't build a metal one?"

"Walker told me that the alpacas weren't comfortable near the metal."

"If that's how they decided to build another wooden barn, then they deserve to have something happen to it," Daed said. "They shouldn't be paying those blasted farm animals any mind at all."

"That's a harsh thing to say," Carl murmured.

"It's misguided, too," Ally added. "The alpacas bring in a lot of money. If the animals aren't content, it doesn't do any of them any good."

His father shrugged. "I can't help how I feel. Besides, we're talking about buildings that protect people in fires and tornados. A wooden barn isn't as safe as a metal one."

Shocked, Carl gazed at their father. When his *daed* picked up a pencil and started working on a crossword, Carl swung his gaze over to the other members of the family.

Kevin and Ally exchanged glances, and their mother looked upset but kept silent.

It seemed that was how everyone handled his father now. They let Daed spout off rude things and didn't correct him. Carl supposed that approach kept the peace, but he found it irritating.

The wind picked up, and the sky darkened. Small dots of hail fell from the sky. Every once in a while, they'd ping against the windows. He listened to the wind, wishing once again that there was a bigger window so he could see just how bad the sky looked.

When his father picked up the *Budget*, opening to another page with a snap of the newsprint, it grated on him. Carl knew then that it was time to make a choice. He could either pretend his father's words weren't offensive—or he could speak his mind.

As far as he was concerned, there was only one choice.

"I think you're wrong," he said at last.

His father's eyebrows pulled together as he lowered the paper yet again. "Excuse me?"

"You heard me, Daed. Ever since I've returned, I've had to listen to you spout off insults about the Schotts. Even though I've moved on and am fine, you continue to bear a grudge against them."

"You almost died."

"I did, but that wasn't their fault. Lightning hit the barn."

Dropping the paper on his lap, Daed crossed his arms over his chest. "Carl, that is not the whole story, and you know it."

"I do know it. I was there. Obviously."

"Do we have to talk about this right now? A tornado is practically over our heads!" Mamm exclaimed before lowering her voice. "Carl, discussing the fire isn't going to change the past, you know."

"I don't need it changed, but I am uncomfortable with the way Daed has turned the event into something that it wasn't."

"What are you talking about? It was a fire in the Schotts' barn. You were covered in burns and have gone through countless hours of pain and suffering while they got off scot-free. They don't even act like it was their fault."

"Because it wasn't. The fire was caused by a bolt of lightning."

"Their daughter lured you there. May had no shame. If she had conducted herself modestly, then you would still be fine."

Carl tried to control his temper. A dozen replies filled his head, but he didn't want to say something that he would always regret.

But then Ally spoke. "You are wrong, Father. You have twisted everything into so many knots, I doubt even the Lord himself could straighten them out."

"Don't speak about the Lord that way," Mamm chided.

"I don't think the Lord is having any problem with me trying to talk some sense into you two," Ally retorted. "The Schotts are part of my family now. Daed, it's awful that you're trying to make a tragedy into something worse by disparaging May's character."

"It can't be helped. She met with a boy alone when she was only sixteen years old. Her behavior was shameful."

Each one of his father's words made Carl flinch. "Don't speak about May like that. She and I were close. Yes, we might have broken some rules, but we didn't do anything shameful."

"You might have once admired her, but I think it's obvious that she doesn't deserve your admiration. Honestly, I'm surprised you have anything to do with her at all, Carl."

Their mother put down her project. "Able, stop. You are being cruel."

"What, now you are saying you don't agree with me either?"

She looked down at her lap. "*Nee*, I am not saying that."

Kevin stood up. "But you are, Mamm. It's been easier for you to blame May instead of the fact that the fire was a terrible accident."

"Or me, because I was in the barn with her."

"You shouldn't have been there, Carl, but you were older."

There was no way he was going to let them twist the truth. "I was only a year older. However, if I was older, then I should've known better, right?"

Mamm's eyes filled with confusion before she blinked it away. "I don't think we should talk about the past any longer. It doesn't do any of us any good."

Carl shook his head. "We can stop for now, but I am not going to pretend this conversation didn't take place. Actually—"

A roar shook the room, cutting his words off like a buzz saw. His mother gasped, and his father's newspaper fell to the floor.

It seemed the warnings had been correct. The tornado had come.

The whole house seemed to be getting beaten with a giant's fist, determined to shake them out.

Ally reached for Carl's hand.

He pulled her into his arms and sank down on the couch next to their mother. Kevin was sitting on the floor, his arms wrapped around his knees. Their father was on the other couch with his head bowed—obviously praying hard.

Carl knew he should be doing the very same thing, but he couldn't seem to relax enough to reach out to the One who could help them most.

Instead, while he continued to hold his sister, a myriad of awful scenarios rattled around in his head. All his worst fears kept popping up. What would he do if the house was hit? If his truck was ruined?

What if the Schotts fared worse . . . or, if his worst fears were realized, something happened to May?

As if she'd felt him tense, Ally pulled away from him. "It's gonna be okay. It has to. I just got married."

Her whisper was a soothing balm as the air turned dark and the rain and hail seemed to switch directions and pelt them from the other side.

Realizing Ally was waiting for him to respond, he cleared his throat. "I know, Al. We'll pray for Walker and May and their parents. But we canna let negative thoughts take hold of us, right? We need to give thanks that the five of us are all together. That is something we can be grateful for."

"I . . . I suppose so."

"I know so. And don't forget, God is here, too. He might not be able to save us from a tornado—but He is here in other ways, right? I'm sure of it." When Ally's tension eased, Carl exhaled in relief. He also drew comfort from the knowledge that while the Lord might not be able to save them from harm—any more than He had saved him and May from a lightning bolt—He would give them strength.

The Lord had also brought Carl home at long last. If he hadn't decided to finally come back to Apple Creek for a spell, he would've only heard about the storm after the fact. It would be a piece of news on his computer. Or worse, part of a weekly phone call, something that his mother might have mentioned but made light of so he wouldn't worry.

Feeling relieved and finally at peace, he bowed his head and prayed beside his family. There was so much to be thankful for, and so much to give praise for.

It was time he stopped wishing things that had happened were different. It was time to give thanks for what was happening in the present.

That was enough.

Chapter 30

Nestled in the storm cellar, May, Walker, and their mother were on their feet, staring through the small window in the cellar door. The tornado had passed, and the worst of the rain seemed to have lessened as well.

For the last fifteen minutes, all they had heard was light rain falling.

The air in the cellar felt thick with tension. May knew that her brother and her mother were as worried as she was. There was a cloying sense of desperation surrounding them. Never had she wished more that they had a radio or a phone with them. She wanted some way to learn what was happening outside and in the rest of Apple Creek. Had the storm completely passed, or were they simply between bouts of chaos? It seemed only God knew. As always, only God knew what was in their future—and what was in their hearts.

All at once, nothing about the past seemed to matter anymore. Not the scars or the guilt or the secrets. Not even the regrets.

Maybe most especially not the regrets. Preacher Elias had

once told her that regrets were the baggage of sinners. If one was carrying them around and refusing to give up their burden to the Lord, then one's faith wasn't strong enough.

May had never truly believed that. She'd always thought it was rather high-handed of Preacher Elias to believe that it was easy to cast away regret and move forward.

But now, faced with the loss of all their animals and their home? She finally understood. She wished she could go back through the last six years and not give so much significance to that fire. She wished she had not felt so guilty for being afraid. She wished she had given herself some grace instead of finding fault with the actions of a sixteen-year-old. She wished she had simply told her family the truth and put the event behind her.

Now, as the whole world seemed to fall silent, she vowed to do just that.

As another few moments passed and even the rain seemed to go quiet, her mother reached for the door. "I think it's time we looked around. Walker, what do you think?"

"I think you're right." He loosened the latch. "Let's open it up."

"I can help," May said. She moved to stand beside her brother and helped to push open the door. At first, it didn't seem to budge.

"I think something's covering it," Walker muttered. "Come on, May. Let's give it another go."

She pulled over a small stool and hopped on it. Placed her hands on the wood. "I'm ready when you are."

"Okay. One. Two. Three!"

Together they pushed with all their might. The wet wood groaned. Walker's muscles bunched with the strain. "Almost."

May stepped closer; then their mother added her strength, too.

At last, the door creaked open. A tree limb fell to the side as a burst of fresh, clean air rushed inside. May breathed deep.

Walker edged up the ladder and poked his head out.

"What do you see?" Mamm asked. "The house? Is it there?"

"*Jah*, it is there. It looks fine."

"Yay!" May hugged her mother.

Her mother had tears in her eyes. "*Jah*. What a blessing. Praise the Lord."

Walker climbed the rest of the way out. "So, there's debris everywhere," he called down. "But the roof looks good. And the yard. Oh!"

Even from the depths of the cellar, May could hear her brother's shock.

Quickly Mamm climbed up. "Oh no. Oh, *nee*!"

When the ladder was clear, May climbed up at last. A light rain fell on her skin. The air smelled like freshly turned soil. She inhaled deeply.

The first thing she noticed was their front porch swing in pieces. Then she saw two fallen limbs of the oak tree.

Quickly, her gaze darted to the house. It was still standing and looked as if it hadn't sustained too much damage beyond the porch swing and a few broken windows.

At last, gathering her courage, she turned toward the barn.

And realized that half of it was gone.

It was as if a giant had taken a knife and neatly cut it in two and disposed of half of it. Her mind seemed to be playing tricks on her. That's what it felt like as she ran toward the barn, followed by the rest of the family. Her eyes kept scanning the area, taking in snippets of what she saw but not really processing them.

A couple of chickens squawked. Three were wandering in the field. Their feathers looked rumpled. Honestly, they looked just as confused as she felt as they pecked at the ground.

Their cow was standing in the barn. Though the back wall was gone, she was still in her roomy stall, her big brown eyes looking sadder than ever. She let out a mournful moo.

Her *mamm* ran to Jack and Jill, their plow horses and put her arms around Jill's neck and ran a hand along her flank. The sight was surprising. Her mother always said that the horse was just a farm animal, not a pet. Now, though, she was obviously hugging her. But May wasn't sure whether her mother was caressing the horse in order to comfort it — or if she was seeking comfort from the animal.

Only then was she finally able to allow herself to peer into the back of the barn at the alpacas. Walker had joined them and was speaking slowly.

"Everything is all right now," he murmured. "The storm has passed and you are safe now."

Unfortunately, the little furry group wasn't moving. Several were making high-pitched cries. They seemed to be so frightened that they were afraid to move. Well, she could certainly relate to that.

Finally wrapping her head around the situation, May hurried forward as best she could through the debris left by the storm.

"How are they?" May called out. "Are any of them injured?" Her mind started to race. She had no idea how she was going to be able to get the vet over to the farm under these circumstances.

Walker turned her way, his eyes sad. "I think we lost Dancer, May."

"Are you sure?"

He nodded. "She's not here. If she was anywhere nearby, you know the others would be grouped around her."

"You're right." Crushed, she bit her lip as she hurried closer. Stepping over a jagged piece of sheet metal, she scanned the broken sides of the barn—and the land surrounding them. Broken branches, uprooted trees, huge pieces of wood and metal littered the ground. As painful as it was to do, she forced herself to examine everything more closely. Looking for Dancer's lifeless white body. "She's dead?"

Eyes looking vacant, Walker shrugged. "I couldn't say. She's simply gone."

That didn't make sense. "What are you saying? Dancer ran off on her own?"

Walker made a disparaging sound. "Come on, May. Look around you. Obviously, not all these trees and debris are from our property. The tornado could've carried her body away."

The thought of the terrible tornado sweeping up the little alpaca was horrifying. Some of the tears she'd been trying so hard to hide slid down her cheeks. She didn't bother wiping them away. "Poor Dancer! What should we do? Should I go search for her?"

Her brother swallowed. "We canna think about her right now. We've got to concentrate on the others. They're in a bad way."

As May approached, she noticed how tightly the animals were huddled together. Honestly, they couldn't be any closer if their bridles had been clipped together. It was obvious that they were scared to death and afraid to leave their friends.

Only Comet was gazing at her. His long black eyelashes framed his eyes as he stared at her intently, as if to ask her how she was going to make everything better.

May had no idea.

It was as if all the information her brain was getting was blocked. As if her mind refused to accept what she saw. It was too much to take in. She felt dizzy.

"I don't know where to put them," she blurted. Of course, the moment she said the words, she wished she could take them back. She needed to be helpful, not needy.

Her mother seemed to understand. "The corral is still standing. Get them over to the pen, May. They need to be contained so Walker can figure out what is still salvageable in the barn. Can you do that?"

"Of course." But staring at the little group, she drew a blank. She knew them well. Alpacas were scared of just about everything. They also thrived on stability and routine. They weren't going to go anyplace where they didn't feel safe. And they didn't feel safe at the moment because they were missing Dancer. Vibrant, bossy, gregarious Dancer. "How am I going to get you all to move to the pen?" she murmured to herself.

"Figure it out, May," Mamm said, her voice hoarse. "I need to check on the house. Oh, where is your father? I'm afraid some of the back windows are broken. I need to see if the gas lines are all right and if there's any damage inside."

When their mother walked away, she noticed that Walker kept staring out at the open field. "Are you worried that Dancer went that way? If she ran, I think she'll be all right," May said with more confidence than she felt. "There aren't any creeks that way."

Walker frowned at her. "I'm not thinking about an alpaca, May. I'm wondering what happened over at the Hiltys'. It's killing me, not knowing about Ally." He clenched his fists. "If something happened to her while I was here in our storm shelter, I won't ever forgive myself."

"Oh, Walker. I'm sorry. Of course, you're worried." When he continued to gaze across the field, she said, "Do you think the tornado could've hit their house, too?"

He nodded. "Why wouldn't it? There's every possibility."

"Yes. I . . . I guess you're right." Another wave of panic seized her. What had happened to the little town of Apple Creek? How much damage had been done to their friends' houses? Had some people lost more than just their live-stock? She closed her eyes and prayed again. She couldn't change the past, of course, but the Lord could at least give everyone the strength to bear the pain.

He sighed. "Well, come on. I'll help you get these guys out to the corral. They're not going to like standing in the rain, but it ain't like they'd be much drier over here any-way."

Only then did May realize that the rain continued to fall. She was soaked to the skin and hadn't even realized it. Iron-ically, that fact seemed to give her the shot of courage she'd been searching for. She looked back at the alpacas. Comet stared back at her; the white mark on his forehead looked like a lightning bolt.

Given the day's events, the fact that it was this particular alpaca that was silently encouraging her seemed fitting.

"*Nee*, Walker, I've got this. You worry about the barn and the animals' food. Or you can go to the Hiltys' house if you want. Mamm and Daed will understand. I certainly do."

"I'm not going to go over there yet. Running around just to see how Ally is doing won't help anything but my heart. She's likely doing the same thing you and I are—helping her parents take stock." He swallowed. "I will let you look after the alpacas, though. I fear I don't have the patience for their antics right now."

When he walked away, she met Comet's eyes again and then remembered that Comet was always trying to be the alpha alpaca. Maybe if she gave him this chance, he would prove that he was worthy of the position.

After scooping up a small paper bag of treats, she walked to his side. "Comet, come with me, if you please."

Comet blinked but didn't move.

"You can do this, Comet. You can be strong and brave and a leader. I feel sure of it."

Just as if he completely understood, Comet picked up a hoof and pawed at the ground.

"*Gut* job, Comet." She gave him a treat. Noticing that the other alpacas were slowly starting to realize that Comet was thinking about moving, May nodded. "That's right, everyone. Comet is going to do a *gut* job."

Vixen and Dasher, the two youngest alpacas, hummed, showing that they were interested and happier.

That vote of approval seemed to be the bit of encouragement Comet needed. He stepped toward May.

"*Danke*, Comet, come along now," she added, keeping her voice kind, yet firm. Then she started walking toward the corral. A few seconds later, Comet followed her. Then Prancer followed him. Then Blitzen and Donner. And then the rest.

Each of them carefully followed May and Comet as if they were playing follow the leader. Perhaps that was exactly what they were doing.

Ten minutes later, she was giving treats to each alpaca, murmuring encouraging words, and then finally closing the gate behind them.

She'd done it. In the grand scheme of things, she knew it wasn't much at all. But for herself—and for her little furry friends, it was something huge. They'd each shown that they could pick themselves up and do what was expected.

It was something to be proud of.

Chapter 31

The tornado had passed into the next county and eventually dissipated. Miraculously, the wind had died away. Though it was raining, the sky no longer looked as frightening. The twister had either lost steam or moved on to cause destruction someplace else.

Though she didn't wish anyone harm, Ally found she didn't care what happened to the tornado—or what was happening in other towns around the area. All that mattered at the moment was that the storm had passed and her family's house was still standing.

Now all she had to do was hope that the Schotts had been as blessed—and that Walker would soon arrive to retrieve her. Thinking that she was waiting for her husband to come get her made Ally smile. They might have only been married a few weeks, but her priorities had already shifted. Now, though she loved her family as much as ever, she didn't feel that she belonged here. Instead, she belonged by Walker's side. Wherever he was, she wanted to be there, too. In the meantime, Ally knew she needed to help her brothers and her parents as much as possible.

She'd gone out with her father to inspect the barn. Mamm had been so shaken up by the storm, and likely their argument, that Kevin had elected to stay by her side and help her put the basement back in order. Ally knew he was the right person for that task. He was more patient with their mother than she was these days.

Daed tapped the side of the barn and grinned. "This steel was worth every penny. Look how well it weathered the storm. Tons of tree limbs stuck to it, but I don't even see a dent in the siding."

Though part of her wanted to roll her eyes at his attempt to remind her that he had been right about building a metal barn instead of a wooden one, Ally didn't want to argue with him again or pick a fight. "It is certainly in fine shape," she said. When he didn't look exactly pleased with her faint praise, she added, "I mean, it's in excellent shape. It looks practically new."

"*Danke*, daughter."

Knowing that he was thanking her for more than just her compliments about the barn, Ally smiled at her father. "Let's go see how the animals fared."

Walking with a new spring in his step, her father nodded. "*Jah*. They'll be wanting some reassurance, I reckon. Blossom, the most. Anything untoward seems to upset her milk."

Sure enough, when he entered the barn, every one of the animals looked their way. It was obvious that they were shaken up.

She rushed over to their stalls. "I know," she murmured soothingly as she walked down the row, reaching out and gently rubbing and petting each critter. "It was frightening, but things are better now. The storm has passed."

Blossom continued to moo mournfully. The gelding was pawing the ground with a hoof, but her father was talking to him in an easy, gentle tone. When the horse calmed, her *daed* gave him oats and rubbed his side.

Ally did the same thing with the plow horses, though they seemed to be the calmest of the lot.

Thirty minutes later, they walked back out. "They weathered the storm as well as could be expected," Daed said.

She smiled up at him. "I agree. We are blessed."

"Indeed." He looked as if he was about to add something, but noticed Carl, Kevin, and her mother at the same time she did.

Ally noticed they were standing in a semicircle, staring at something in the back field. "I wonder what could have happened over there?"

"We'd best go see."

Together, they strode through the corn field to the one where they grew alfalfa.

"What happened?" Daed asked when they reached the rest of the family. "Did something land in the field?"

"I guess you could say that," Kevin said.

When she was finally able to see what they were staring at, Ally gaped. It was one of the Schotts' alpacas. A pure white one was standing in the battered alfalfa field, looking alone and very afraid. "Oh no," she murmured.

"Poor little thing. She sure looks lost and scared, don't she?" Mamm asked.

"She must have gotten scared and run," Kevin said. "That doesn't make much sense, though. Even I know alpacas hate to be alone."

"That's Dancer," Ally said. "She's easy to identify because she's snow white."

"She is a pretty thing," Mamm murmured.

"I've been trying to think of a way to get it to come with me," Carl said, "but every option seems like a bad idea. If I try to fasten a lead around its neck, it's liable to fight me."

"We're going to have to get either Walker or May to come over for it," Mamm said. "I don't know how, though."

"I'll go over there and talk to Walker," Ally said. "I want to see him, anyway."

Their father frowned. "You don't think you should wait for him to come to you?"

"*Nee.* If Dancer has come all the way over here, something must be very wrong. She wouldn't have left the others if she had a choice."

"I agree," Carl said. "We need to go over there now. Something could've happened to May."

"I can understand Ally needing to get to her husband, but I don't want you running over to May, Carl," their father said.

But it was obvious that Carl wasn't going to put up with their father's directive for even a moment. "Don't tell me what to do. May and I aren't your business, Daed."

"Of course, you are. You're still my son."

"I am, but I'm also a grown man."

Stubborn as ever, Daed patted Carl's shoulder. "Now listen, son, you have to be careful, right? You shouldn't give her any more ideas. You don't want to have anything to do with her in the future."

"Of course, I do. Don't you understand what's happened? We're all family now. May and I have become close again."

"How close?" Mamm asked.

"Very close."

Mamm gave him a pointed look. "Carl, I noticed you talking to her at the wedding, but I didn't think there was anything beyond that. Have you two been sneaking around?"

"I'm too old to sneak, Mother."

"Don't get snippy. I'm really just trying to understand what's been going on. Now, tell me the truth. Are Ben and Marjorie encouraging this match? Is that where this is coming from?"

Ally stared at her mother. "Mamm, you are being ridiculous. Carl is going to talk to and see whomever he wants. He's English now and has been living on his own for years."

"Yet he's keeping company with May once again."

"So what? Mamm, are you jealous of Marjorie and Ben? Are you worried that they'll get closer to Carl than you are?"

Her cheeks turned pink. "Of course not. But I am worried that Marjorie Schott is encouraging a match that has no future."

Ally glanced at Carl. Since it was obvious that he was trying hard to keep his temper in check, she continued to try to make their mother see reason. "Of course, May and Carl can have a future if that's what they want. Why, look at what happened to me. Walker and I are already married. And we almost got married without your blessing."

Her mother's expression looked almost as frantic as the animals' when she and her father had first entered the barn. Ally knew that her mother was desperately trying to keep some control over her two oldest children. But it was a useless attempt. Maybe on another day Ally would have had patience with it, but not now. Certainly not less than an hour after they'd survived a tornado.

"Ally, as much as I appreciate you standing up for me, we need to stop talking," Carl said. "This little alpaca is scared to death. We need to get her back to the herd—or at the very least, get Walker or May over here to take her home. Plus, there might be more animals wandering around."

"Carl's right," Ally said. "Mamm, Daed, it's time to stop clinging to a hate that is only going to tear you down. If you continue to put up walls, you're going to lose me."

"Well said, Ally," Kevin put in.

Their father turned to Kevin with a frown. "You're on their side now?"

"Daed, I'm on our family's side. I just want everyone to get along."

Kevin's words broke Ally's heart. Their little brother had been dealing with this feud from the time he was ten years old. "Mamm, Daed, I'm going to tell you this from the bottom of my heart. It's time you both stopped trying to make us do things we don't want to do and opened your eyes to the rest of our blessings. Stop being angry about Carl when Carl has long since decided not to be a victim."

"Are you ready, Ally?" Carl said. "I'll walk over with ya."

"I'm ready. Let's go."

When they got to the alpaca's side, it tensed and skittered backward. "Won't you come with us, Dancer?" Ally asked in her sweetest voice.

Dancer wouldn't even look at her.

"I promise, all we want to do is return you to the rest of your alpaca clan. Don't you want to see Prancer, Vixen, Dasher, and the rest?"

Dancer's head went up, showing she recognized the names. But she didn't move one inch.

Ally realized then that the little alpaca wasn't going to let them lead her anywhere. She was scared and skittish—and who could blame her? Somehow she'd gotten all the way over to their property in the middle of the storm.

"Maybe Dancer will follow us?" Carl murmured as they walked on.

Ally looked behind her. The white alpaca was gazing at them but hadn't moved. "Kevin, stay with her, wouldya?"

"*Jah*, sure."

"*Danke, bruder*," Carl said. "I'll be back soon."

"No worries. I've got this," Kevin called back, making Ally giggle.

"I think our little brother is growing up, Carl."

Glancing Kevin's way, Carl nodded. "I agree. It's a blessing, too. If our parents continue to be such a handful, we're going to need all the help we can get."

Unable to stop herself, Ally giggled again. Carl was exactly right.

Chapter 32

When they were out of sight of their house, Carl exhaled in relief. He loved his parents dearly, but he didn't enjoy battling with them about their relationship with the Schott family. He'd naïvely imagined that Ally and Walker's marriage would finally smooth things over, but it was now obvious that their *mamm* and *daed* were determined to continue the feud as long as possible.

"Ally, these parents of ours can be aggravating."

"Oh, I know."

"Are you doing okay?" His sister's heart had to be feeling battered by their parents' disapproval now that she and Walker were married.

Ally lifted a shoulder. "I'm trying to be all right, but it's hard. I love Mamm and Daed, but it they're determined to find fault with Walker and May, I'm going to have to distance myself from them. That's going to be really hard. I don't want to do that, but I need to follow my heart."

Carl didn't have all the answers, but he did know what to say in response. "You do. This continued feud is their choice, not ours. We've asked them to let it go but they won't."

"You're right."

"When I go back to live in Cleveland full-time, I'm going to have to make sure I reach out to Kevin a lot. Otherwise, he'll adopt their attitude just to keep the peace."

"I agree." She paused, as if choosing her words. "As much as I love our parents, I'm not blind to their faults. And as much as I love Walker, I am realistic enough to see that I can't pretend the conflict between our families doesn't exist. I think you're in the same spot."

"I am. I might not like how our parents are acting, but if they won't change it's going to hurt."

She sighed. "I keep hoping that the Lord will answer my prayers. I really need Him to intervene and resolve this conflict. One day, I hope he'll listen to me."

Holding her elbow to help her over a fallen tree branch, Carl spoke. "God doesn't work that way, Ally. He doesn't come around with a tool kit and fix our problems."

She frowned. "I never mentioned a tool kit."

"You know what I mean. He doesn't go around and fix things when we ask."

Ally didn't look happy as her footsteps slowed. "How can you be so sure? He works miracles all the time."

"I know He does. But I also realize that there are plenty of times when people have asked for an instant miracle, and it doesn't happen. But that doesn't mean He's ignoring us."

"I had no idea you had so many strong feelings about the Lord and His ways."

"I don't know if I do or I don't. All I do know is that I feel like I got pretty close to Him when I was living alone and going through all those surgeries." Feeling vulnerable, both because he was daring to mention how difficult it had been to be alone so much, and how he'd developed a relationship with the Lord, Carl swallowed hard. "I can't tell you how many times I used to pray for Him to make me look normal again, but He never did."

Her expression fell. "Carl—"

"*Nee*, let me finish." He released a breath he hadn't even realized he'd been holding. "Ally, what I learned was that even though God didn't 'fix' me, He gave me something better. He helped me find a way to manage the pain I was feeling. He gave me doctors and nurses and physical therapists. He even provided therapists for my heart and my head. When I cried, He made sure I wasn't alone by staffing the hospitals with chaplains and volunteers."

Feeling as if he'd laid himself bare, he added, "What I'm trying to say is that He did hear my prayers, but the solution wasn't the one I thought I wanted. It was the one I needed. I didn't need to have pain and sadness removed from my life . . . I just needed a way to manage them."

Uncomfortably aware that his sister was staring at him as if he was a stranger, Carl rolled his shoulders. "So that was a lesson for me to learn. I didn't mean to sound so preachy, though. I'm sorry for that."

"*Nee*. Don't be sorry." She reached for his hand. Her soft, slim one curved around his scarred left palm as if there was nothing wrong with it at all. "Carl, I . . . well, I guess I never really thought about what your life was like up in Cleveland. I feel terrible that you were alone so much. I should've made Mamm hire a driver to take me to you. We could have played games or something while you were stuck in bed."

"There was no reason for you to be there. I couldn't have played many games anyway." Once again, he was so glad that his sister had no idea about how bad those months had been. He'd almost always been either bandaged up or work-

198 *Shelley Shepard Gray*

ing on his injured limbs to regain muscle tone. Neither the recovery nor the physical therapy had been easy, and he'd been on a lot of painkillers. If she'd seen him that way, the memory would have always stayed in her mind. He would've hated that.

"But still, I could have helped take care of you. Even if it was just reading you books or something. You're my brother."

"I'm your older brother."

"That doesn't make a difference."

"In my mind it did . . . and it still does. I'm supposed to look after you, not the other way around."

"Maybe we all should've moved to be near you. I wish we had."

He chuckled. "Ally, that's sweet of you to say, but it wasn't possible. A bunch of Amish people living in downtown Cleveland near the Cleveland Clinic? Even if you put aside the fact that Daed had a farm to take care of and you and Kevin were in school, I think living in a rental unit or at the Ronald McDonald House would've gotten old really quick," he teased.

"It might have at that."

He chuckled. "In any case, you're missing the point I was trying to make, which was that you can pray to God to fix all your problems, but He might respond by giving you the tools to fix them yourself."

"And if He does, then those tools will help more in the long run than just a quick fix."

He nodded. "Yes. Hopefully."

Ally pursed her lips. She stayed quiet for a few moments, obviously thinking about his words as they walked. "I guess I never thought about that, but you're right," she said at last. She was about to add something more when they reached the crest of the hill between the two properties. They looked down. "Oh, no!"

Carl stopped abruptly by her side. "I can't believe it. Look at the Schotts' barn."

Ally's expression matched the dismay he was feeling. "The side of it is shredded!" she exclaimed. "I . . . I've never seen anything like it."

Neither had he. "I hope the rest of the animals didn't die. There's debris everywhere."

Ally increased her pace as they headed down the hill. "I bet Walker and his parents are so upset. They're going to need a lot of help getting that barn fixed."

"Not fixed, Ally. They're going to need a brand-new barn. A whole barn raising."

"For a second time." She smiled. "I think a real barn raising is going to be great fun, don't you? It's been years since I went to a barn raising."

"I don't remember if I've ever been to one."

"That's because you haven't. There've only been two in the last six years, and one of them was right here. It's about time you went to one."

"I hope I can make this one." He wanted to help the Schott family, of course, but he really wanted to be there for May.

"I hope so, too." Ally smiled. "I'm going to take your advice to heart and start talking to people about how to organize it."

He playfully slapped a hand against his forehead. "Uh oh. I have a feeling I've created a monster."

She chuckled. "Not at all. But thinking about everything you went through on your own made me realize that I've been so focused on myself and Walker . . . I have forgotten that our problems are not insurmountable. Daed and Mamm might not like Walker's parents, but that is their choice.

Lying about my feelings isn't the best way to handle things, ain't so? Two wrongs don't make a right."

Ally probably didn't realize it, but she was spouting all kinds of sayings that their father loved to proclaim. Just as Carl was about to tease her about that, he spied May standing in her driveway. She was wearing a blue dress and a white *kapp* and white tennis shoes. The rest of her hardly looked familiar at all. Instead of appearing her usual happy self, she looked completely alone and lost.

When she met his gaze, she started crying.

"Uh oh," he murmured. Releasing Ally's hand, he strode forward. He had only one goal in mind—to get to May's side as quickly as possible. "What's wrong?" he murmured. Of course, as soon as he asked, he wished he could have taken back the words. What wasn't wrong?

"Everything." She hiccupped, then covered her face with her hands as if she was ashamed of herself.

"May! May, hey," he murmured softly as he pulled her into his arms. She wrapped her arms around his neck, and their connection felt comfortable, so right. "It's okay."

"Oh, Carl. I don't know if anything is." Tears streaming down her face, she leaned in closer.

He continued to murmur nonsense words as he attempted to soothe her, rubbing her back with care and pressing his lips to her cheek. "I know it's hard, but you're all right, and so am I, yes?"

When she nodded, he leaned back slightly so she could see his face. "How is your family?"

"We're okay. My *daed* was at the neighbors' during the storm, but he's back. Mamm, Walker, and I had to stay in the storm shelter. How is your family?"

"We're all okay, too. So that's our blessing, right? If we are all okay, then we'll get through this."

"I hope so." She bit her lip and then blurted, "Carl, I'm so glad you're here. I don't know what I would've done without you."

"That's not something you have to worry about, May. I am right here."

She released a ragged sigh and nodded. "*Jah*. For now."

Her words stung. Not because she wasn't right but because he was starting to think that simply being back in Apple Creek with May for a short time wasn't going to be enough. Not for him and not for them.

"Please don't worry," he said. "I'm going to be here tomorrow and the next day."

Some of the light dimmed in her eyes. It was obvious that her mind had drifted to the obvious conclusion.

What about the day after that? Or next week or next month? What was she going to do then?

Chapter 33

May had never been so glad to see Carl. She stayed by his side as they walked closer to the remains of the barn. She needed his support and wanted to support him, too. Surely the tornado had shaken him up as much as it had rattled her entire family.

Vaguely aware of Walker pulling Ally into his arms, she reached for Carl's hand. "I'm so, so glad to see you, but I'm surprised, too. Is there a reason you've come, beyond returning Ally to Walker?"

Carl glanced over at Ally and Walker. They looked even less aware of the rest of the family than she was. "First of all, we wanted to make sure you were all right. But there's another reason we came, too."

"What is that?"

"We have something of yours."

Her parents were close enough to hear. "What is that?" Daed asked. "Another piece of our barn?"

Carl smiled at that. "Kind of. Hey, Ally? Want to break away from your husband for a moment and help me out?"

"Jah." Holding Walker's hand, they walked closer. "We came over to tell you that we did find something that we're fairly sure belongs to you."

"What is it?" Daed asked.

Ally smiled. "We have an alpaca."

To her shock, May's mother started crying. "You found Dancer?"

"We did. Or rather, she found us."

"What does that mean?" Walker asked.

"Your alpaca is standing in our field, and she looks lost," Ally added with a small smile.

"Is she okay? I mean, can she walk?" Walker added.

Carl exchanged glances with his sister. "I thought she was in good shape," he murmured. "What did you think, Ally?"

"I didn't notice any cuts or her limping." Smiling slightly, she added, "Mainly Dancer just looked confused—but stubborn."

May chuckled. "That is Dancer. She's feisty yet shy . . . she likes to pretend to be in charge."

"Well, she's currently in charge of our field," Carl teased. "She's standing there like she owns it." Of course, that was putting things a bit over the top, but he didn't care. He'd continue to lie just a little bit if it meant that May's tears would dry.

Every member of the Schott family seemed to be rejuvenated. "Your news is such a blessing," Marjorie said. "I'm afraid we all thought the worst had happened to Dancer. You two coming over here to tell us the news . . . well, it lifts my spirits. *Danke.*"

"Jah," Ben added. "Hearing that Dancer is not only alive but unharmed is a miracle. The Lord is so good. It's certainly a blessing that we didn't expect to hear."

Ally smiled at Walker. "Believe it or not, we actually tried to lead her over, but she wouldn't have anything to do with us."

May nodded in sympathy. "Alpacas don't make friends very easily. They're scared of most everything, you know."

"If one of you came over, would she go with you?"

"*Jah*," Walker said. "I'll walk over with ya both."

"I want to come, too," May said, looking hesitant for the first time. "If that's okay?"

"Of course, it is," Carl said. "We need your help."

May, like her mom, started crying.

Before he thought the better of showing so much affection in front of her parents and brother, Carl pulled her into his arms again. When she clung to him, he knew it was the right decision. "Hey now, I'm sorry. I promise, I didn't mean to upset you."

"I'm not upset. These are happy tears. Really good tears. The best tears." She beamed at him.

He wasn't sure about that, but he didn't want to argue.

"I'm afraid you're going to have to get used to emotion if you want to come calling on May," Ben quipped. "Though I canna say I blame her. I might start bawling like a baby, too. You see, we thought Dancer had died. That the tornado had pulled her into the air or something."

"I'm glad that wasn't the case, though it is a mystery how she ended up so far away when the rest of the herd stayed in the barn."

Ally pressed a hand to her lips. "I'm sorry, I didn't even ask. How are the other animals?"

"Besides a few chickens, they all survived. The other seven alpacas were huddled together in a back corner of the barn. They were scared to death but otherwise doing okay."

Walker reached out for Ally's hand. "Come on, let's go find a bridle and a lead. Some of the tack is scattered around the yard, but most of it is still in the barn."

When they walked away, Carl whispered to May, "Are you feeling better now?"

"I think so." Looking awkward but determined, she stepped toward her parents. "Mamm, Daed, I don't know if you've had the opportunity to say much to Carl during the wedding."

After a pause, her parents walked over.

"It's a blessing to see you doing so well, Carl. We prayed for you often."

"*Danke.*"

"I appreciate that."

"I would say that I hope we can all get along one day, but I have a feeling that sentiment is a little late. It's obvious that you and May have gotten close again without any assistance from us."

"I don't think it's too late at all. The Lord has obviously been trying to remind me that there's no time limit on friendship—or the feelings in one's heart."

May looked up at him with a tender expression. "I couldn't have said that better."

"Walker has already told us what he thinks about our two families barely talking for years and years. I hope one day maybe there will be hope for all of us to get along like we used to."

She was talking about his parents, of course. "I hope and pray the same thing," Carl said.

Walker and Ally joined them, a bridle and lead in Walker's hands. "We're ready if you are."

"*Jah.*" Looking at Ben and Marjorie, Carl said, "I'll be back to help with the barn tomorrow."

"That ain't necessary," Ben said.

"It is," Ally added. "*Mei bruder* and I have decided that we are done with this feud. We're going to move forward and live our lives. If our parents refuse to go along with us, then that is going to be their loss."

"If the Lord can keep half a barn together in the middle of a tornado—take care of us and even find a way to help Dancer, well, I'm certain that He will be able to find a way to mend a friendship, too," Ben said.

"We'll be back soon with Dancer," Walker said.

"We'll be here. Take your time."

As the four of them set off, Walker and Ally in the lead, May said, "I still can't believe what just happened. You held me in your arms, and my parents didn't say a word."

He chuckled. "They must be in shock from the storm."

"They're not that shocked."

"Hmm. Maybe they think I've become a heathen with my English ways?" He wouldn't call himself a heathen, but he was used to being around people who were a lot more open about PDA.

As she looked up at him, her eyes sparkled. "*Jah*, that must be it."

"If that is the case, are you upset?" They hadn't talked about the future yet. While he hadn't hidden the fact that he now lived his life with two feet in the English world, she might have been hoping that he would give everything up and become Amish again.

As they continued their walk, carefully dodging both muddy spots and discarded debris and tree limbs, May seemed to think about his question. At last, she answered. "While I don't exactly think being a heathen is a good thing, Carl, I don't expect you to be anyone but yourself."

"Are you sure?"

"I'm positive." She glanced his way, apprehension in her eyes. "Of course, I'm more concerned about your expectations of me."

Carl blinked. He realized that he'd been so consumed with thoughts about his life decisions, he'd conveniently forgotten that May had a future of her own to plan.

"Are you baptized?"

"*Nee*," she replied. "I am not baptized. Not yet."

The new tension that flowed between them was as surprising as the change in conversation. How had they gone from being thankful each was unharmed to giving thanks that their families might soon mend their rift . . . to bringing up May's decision about joining the faith?

"I'm sorry," he blurted.

May didn't say a word. Only looked straight ahead. But it was obvious that they both now had a great many things to consider.

Chapter 34

What was Carl sorry for? Asking about her baptism? The fact that she was still trying to make up her mind?

Or that he was so firmly embedded in the English world, he wasn't ever going to be completely happy as a farmer in Apple Creek?

She could practically feel his unease. A part of her yearned to make it better, but even if she could tell him that she had been leaning away from joining the church for quite some time, it wasn't her place to be so forward. He hadn't asked her to be his wife.

He hadn't even acted as if he wanted to court her.

It also wasn't the time. She had an alpaca to fetch and a barn to worry about.

"I see her, May!" Walker called out.

"How is she?"

"She looks *gut!*"

"Come on, you two lazybones," Ally added. "We're not that much younger than ya."

"We're coming along!" Carl retorted. "Dancer obviously

ain't in no rush to come home. She can wait another minute or two."

"Some things never change, do they?" May mused.

"Nope. Even after being apart all this time, Ally, Kevin, and I still seem to revert back to old habits." He grinned at her. "Let's go see if either you or Walker can encourage Dancer to return to her buddies."

May quickened her pace. When she spied Dancer nudging Walker with her nose and looking exactly like her normal self, a lump formed in her throat. "Oh, she looks so good. Walker, what do you think?"

"I haven't checked everything, but she doesn't seem any the worse for wear. I don't see any scratches on her, and she doesn't seem to be in pain."

Dancer's ears perked up when she approached.

"Hiya, Dance." She carefully patted the alpaca's side. To May's relief and happiness, the alpaca didn't shy away.

"She just relaxed a bit. Stay right there, May," Walker said as he finished adjusting the alpaca bridle on the bridge of the animal's nose and snapped on the lead. "Okay, we're good."

That was her signal that it was time to return home. Emotion filled her heart as she turned to Ally and Carl. "I can't thank you enough for coming to get us."

"Of course," Ally said. "I'm just glad that we had a good story to tell you."

"You're right. It could've been something very different." Turning to her brother, she murmured, "Are you ready, Walker?"

"*Jah*. We'll be seeing you both soon. Ally, you come on home as soon as you finish helping your *mamm*, okay?"

Clicking softly, Walker encouraged Dancer to begin the walk back home.

Luckily, Dancer didn't put up a fight. She seemed happy to be back with familiar people.

The alpaca looked around the entire time they walked, her brown eyes seeming to study everything with a renewed interest. "I can't wait to see her reaction when she's reunited with all her friends," May said.

"Me neither. I'm not sure why or how she ended up being the one who ran away, but if one of the animals did have to go, it's a blessing that it was her."

"I agree. Dancer is both smart and confident. If it had been Cupid, she might not have survived."

"Or Donner. He's a beauty, but not too smart or self-reliant."

May smiled up at him. Folks who didn't have alpacas never seemed to understand just how close owners got to their furry friends.

"I've never told you this, but Dancer reminds me a lot of you, May."

"Really? How so?"

"You are smart and have an independent streak as well."

"That's a nice compliment. What brought that on?"

"You know."

"Are you talking about Carl?"

"Of course. I saw the way he held you. It was intense, like you were the most precious person to him in the world."

Carl had made her feel that way. "I'm glad Mamm and Daed didn't throw a fit about it."

"I don't think they'd dare."

The comment seemed to come out of nowhere. "What do you mean by that?"

"Come on, May. There's only you and me and Dancer here. You don't have to guard every word you say."

"I'm not guarding anything, Walker." Feeling defensive, she added, "Besides, you're the one who had to have a quick wedding."

"Ally says that she's grateful it was fast. She said that if she'd had her way, she would've planned for a solid year and worried about every little detail. All she had time to do was think about being married to me."

Her brother looked so full of himself, she had to laugh. "I'm beginning to think that Ally is going to have her hands full with you."

Walker had the grace to tuck his head. "That's true. I'm not always the easiest person to get along with. I'm trying to be the man she needs me to be, though."

"How do you know?"

"Know what?"

"You know . . . how do you know what type Ally needs?"

"Are you thinking about yourself and Carl?"

She nodded. "He and I have had a lot of conversations about our relationship. Some of them have been really good, but sometimes I feel like I'm a diver jumping into a pool of water. I never know how far to go in."

"Or if you're about to get really hurt?"

"*Jah*. In a lot of ways, Carl is so different now."

"Is he? I thought he seemed pretty much the same as ever."

"He's English now. He's more educated and works on a computer all day and has a lot of friends who have nothing to do with our Amish community. He can have anyone he wants or needs."

"Oh, May. I think you're selling yourself short. He might have a bigger circle of friends, but at the end of the day, he only has eyes for you."

"I don't know about that."

"I appreciate your being modest, but you can be honest, too. I canna help but think that if the Lord put the two of you together years ago and if he brought you back together again, He's trying to tell ya that He knows the two of you are meant to be together. He must approve, too."

"I wish it was that easy."

"It is. You're the one who is making everything so hard. Love is easy, May." He kept his voice light. "For what it's worth, I don't think there's a soul in Apple Creek who would be against you and Carl becoming an official couple."

Her insides felt warm. She liked the idea of everyone knowing that Carl Hilty was her man. But of course, she wouldn't be living in Apple Creek. "Carl isn't going to come back here."

"Not permanently."

"But that means that I won't be staying Old Order Amish."

"I know."

She could tell that Walker was biting his tongue so he wouldn't say anything more. She appreciated that. "I hope the animals will be okay until we get a new barn built."

"They'll have to be. It is May. The weather should be mild, and the dogs will keep watch over them at night."

She nodded. "They'll no doubt be getting full of themselves with their new responsibilities."

He laughed. "No doubt."

As they reached the crest of the hill that divided their property from the Hiltys' farm, they stopped, looking down at the barn and the scattered debris. "When you look at the destruction from here, it's a miracle that none of the animals were killed."

"Or that our house is still standing."

"We have much to be thankful for."

Dancer pulled at her lead. It was obvious that she was eager to get home.

May supposed she was, too. Even though she might not be completely sure what the future held in store for her.

Chapter 35

Two weeks after the tornado hit, almost every person in Apple Creek and the surrounding areas showed up at the Schotts' farm bright and early. It was barn-raising day.

Ally, Preacher Elias, several couples from their church district, and even Keim Lumber over in Charm had organized it all. Seeing Ally's detailed notes, plans, and lists for every work detail had been something of a surprise. Walker had known his new wife excelled at organization, but he hadn't known that she enjoyed it so much.

So much so that every time he'd tried to become involved, she had shooed him away, saying that his interference made things worse instead of better.

Luckily, he'd known her long enough not to take offense. Instead, he'd done what she asked and attempted to stay out of her way.

On a Thursday morning, just as the sun was peeking over the horizon, buggies appeared. They parked in one of the east fields. Kevin Hilty and his friends helped unhitch horses from their buggies and direct them to the hastily erected hitching rail.

Walker stood in the field and helped direct traffic and parking while his father greeted all the men, women, and their toolboxes and baskets heaped high with food, lemonade, tea, sandwiches, cookies, and snack mix.

The day before, several men had come with a rentalcompany truck and erected a large white tent next to the spot where the new barn was going to stand. Now, just like their mothers and grandmothers before them, the women organized the church wagon, which held plates, benches, and the like.

Walker's mother was in the midst of it all, and it was obvious that she was enjoying every minute. Her smile was bright and infectious as she bustled from group to group, joking with teenaged girls, commiserating with longtime friends, and nodding as the elderly women gave advice.

Finally, his sister May was helping the children get organized at their workstations. The littlest *kinner* would remain by their mother's sides. Girls nine and ten would help with the buffet and cleanup. Everyone older volunteered to help take water and such out to the men or served as runners, fetching and carrying tools, nails, and whatever the men asked for.

A week ago, Preacher Elias and Robert Walker had drawn up the plans for the barn, his father working alongside them.

When Preacher Elias arrived, everyone gathered around for his welcome speech and prayer.

"God is so good!" he said. "He never gives us too much to handle or makes us work alone. Look at our community here in Apple Creek!"

Everyone started clapping. A few folks even cheered. Next to Walker, his parents and May smiled. How could they not? Here they were, all together and making the best of the situation. The preacher did not lie—God really was so good. He'd not only blessed them with able bodies and minds, but with many friends who were willing to work hard—and keep up everyone's spirits, too.

Unable to help himself, Walker scanned the crowd. There were almost a hundred people assembled, and that didn't even count the families who were scheduled to arrive in a few hours. They'd take over some of the shifts so the men could have a moment for a meal without halting the work.

Maybe the most surprising of the attendees were Robin and Able Hilty. They not only came ready to work but appeared to be sharing in the upbeat atmosphere. Though they still hadn't come around to the notion that their two families could be close again, Walker realized that that was all right. When he and Ally had made the decision to marry, they'd recognized that the relationship between their families might not ever be warm.

He'd been okay with that, but he'd wondered if Ally was going to have regrets one day. She'd assured him that she'd rather find happiness with him than try to make her parents do something they weren't ready to do.

So it was a pleasant surprise when Carl and Ally both shared that their parents had never once thought about not coming over to help out.

Walker had to give his parents credit, too. While some folks might have expected a long conversation or fervent apologies for holding a grudge for years, all his father had done when Able Hilty arrived was nod and thank the man.

Preacher Elias continued. "Everyone, bow your heads and give thanks for the many blessings He gives to us. Give thanks for our friends, our families, our community, and our many hands. Lord, please bless us with good weather, able bodies, and open hearts. Bless the food that so many hands prepared and the time and talents of each person here."

Silence spread over the assembly as each man, woman, and child did as Preacher Elias bid.

A full minute later, the preacher smiled. "With God's help, let's build a barn!"

Children cheered and several of the men clapped.

He scanned the crowd, looking, as always, for Ally. He found her with the other women. She was in a sunny yellow dress. Her white *kapp*, white tennis shoes, and strawberry-blond hair made her glow in the company of the older widows, who were dressed in dark gray.

As if she felt his gaze on her, she looked up and smiled at him. When he smiled back—no doubt looking as smitten with her as he was—the women around her giggled.

One of the men—a septuagenarian nicknamed Ox—slapped him on the back. "You are as besotted as a new bride, Walker."

"I guess I am. Though it ain't my fault that I canna keep my eyes off Ally," he joked. "After all, she's the prettiest girl here."

Ox smiled warmly. "I told my Bethy the same thing this morning. That's love for you, ain't so? It makes the whole world look beautiful."

"It sure does." He could feel his cheeks heat. He sounded like a smitten boy who'd just discovered girls.

Ox laughed. "You all better keep an eye on Walker Schott, men. He might look like he's ready to climb scaffolding, but really he's got his head in the clouds!"

Of course, all the men around him laughed—and a couple even made a joke or two at his expense. Walker didn't care, though. For far too long, he and Ally had had to hide not only their love for each other, but even the fact that they were friends. Being able to smile at her without feeling afraid that one of their sets of parents would find out was an incredible gift.

"It's good you like my sister," Carl said. "Otherwise she would be unbearable when she comes over to help Mamm."

"I could say the same to you," he quipped.

To his amusement, Carl looked away in embarrassment.

Huh, he and May might be older, but they still had a ways to go to be as comfortable as he and Ally were together. Walker couldn't help but feel a little smug about that.

"Walker, you gonna stand there or help us build your barn?" Daniel, one of his friends, called out.

"I'm on my way!"

Walker put on his tool belt and joined the other men on the ground, building trusses and the outside structure. Soon, the air was filled with the sound of saws cutting wood, hammering, and tossed-out instructions and jokes. The men helped and encouraged each other, too.

Every so often, kids or women would bring by bowls of water with ladles. A worker would dip the ladle into the bowl, take a drink, and then pass it on to the next man. Of course, Ally had even made sure to be the one to give Walker a sip of water, which earned her a kiss on the cheek—and even more jokes from the men.

One hour turned into two and then three. One by one, the trusses rose, and men climbed higher. Walker was no carpenter, but he could wield a hammer just fine. He followed Preacher Elias's lead and did whatever the other man said. Every so often, he'd glance toward his father, who was putting together some wind braces with a group of other men his age—one of whom was Able Hilty.

For so long, his father had seemed frazzled and tense. Walker had blamed the grueling life of a farmer for it. But now he was beginning to think that some of the stress his *daed* had been carrying hadn't been caused by work but by the feud between their families. Ben Schott wasn't the type of man to complain, but Walker wondered if maybe his father had been just as upset about the rift as May and he had been.

Preacher Elias looked over at him with an expression of concern. "Walker, you've gone quiet all of a sudden. Do you need to take a break for a spell?"

"*Nee.* I was just thinking that today is a *gut* day."

Elias's expression warmed. "I know what you mean. I've been thinking the same thing as well. Building a barn does take many hands, but building a good life takes many people. Looking around, seeing all of our friends and the way everyone in our circle was so willing to come together, well, it's a blessing indeed."

"Amen to that," Walker murmured.

Elias patted him on the back before walking to the next section of wood that needed to be stacked and carried to the men up on the rafters. "Help me carry this load, Walker." His warm expression showed Walker that his statement's double meaning had been intentional.

Walker smiled back. That meaning wasn't lost on him.

Chapter 36

The Lord had blessed them with clear skies and warm temperatures. Some might even call it a perfect day for a barn raising.

May figured that might be an apt description, but she had a feeling that she wouldn't remember the mild weather as much as the overall feeling of conviviality among everyone who had gathered. Each person seemed determined to work hard, lift other people's spirits, and celebrate the fact that their town had survived the terrible tornado with no casualties and only a minimum of damage.

Though May would never want to experience a tornado again, she was grateful for everyone's support. It was a wonderful reminder of just how loving and close-knit the Apple Creek Amish community was.

While the men worked on the barn itself, the women were the ones who made the big, one-day construction job possible. Instead of hammering nails, they cooked. Instead of carrying lumber, they carried food and casserole dishes.

And, May noted, instead of sweating in the confines of a

new barn, the women were perspiring just as much in the makeshift portable kitchen in their driveway.

One of the oldest women there, formidable Lovina Stutzman, had even started a running joke among the women about keeping hydrated after her granddaughter Addie had mentioned that she was sweating as much as the men but getting no sympathy for it. Now they all playfully reminded each other to drink lots of water, just as the men were doing.

So it was a wonderful *gut* day. A great day. May stayed busy, thanking and encouraging all the women, helping her mother, locating needed items for the luncheon and supper . . . and keeping a close eye on Carl.

She knew he was fit, but a man who worked in an office five days a week was going to be affected by the strenuousness of a barn raising. She didn't want him to overdo it.

Camille noticed. "Stop looking at Carl Hilty like he's made of spun glass. He is holding his own, May."

"I know he is. I just don't want him to get hurt."

"What are you going to do if you think he's doing too much? March over to the barn and call up to him to get down?"

"Of course not. I would never do that."

"Are you sure?"

"*Jah.*" Though May had secretly contemplated warning Carl about doing too much when they had a private moment. If they ever had a private moment.

"Then stop worrying so much, May."

"I will. It's just . . ."

"You're just wanting to protect him instead of remembering that he might be scarred but he isn't helpless?"

"That wasn't what I was doing." When Camille propped a hand on her hip and raised an eyebrow, May was forced to see her friend's point. "Okay, fine. I might have been doing something like that." She winced. "I guess I have been acting silly. There's nothing I can do to keep him safe."

"No, you can put your trust in him, May. If the positions were reversed, that's what you would want, ain't so?"

"*Jah*. Of course."

She kept Camille's pep talk in mind as she made more lemonade and tea that afternoon. If she was the one building the barn instead of Carl, she'd want him to be proud of her. She was proud of Carl, too. Proud and thankful for his help.

Glad that those emotions were now front and center in her mind, she made a point of smiling more often and telling all the women and men there how grateful she was for their help. Everyone seemed to appreciate her enthusiasm and gratitude.

An hour later, the women were finishing up the lunch service. "May I pour you more tea or lemonade?" May asked Daniel Miller.

"*Danke*, but I am good." He smiled in that kind way of his. "May, I'm going to tell you the same thing I told *mei frau*, Addie. Don't overdo it today. You don't need to wait on everyone hand and foot. Though we appreciate it, there's not a man here who can't pour his own refreshment, ain't so?"

She laughed. "You're right."

Obviously pleased that she was giving his words some consideration, Daniel continued. "You ladies are working hard on all the food. Just as hard as we are on the barn."

"I appreciate your words, but I don't mind serving drinks. It gives me a chance to tell everyone how grateful I am for their help."

Daniel waved a hand. "Obviously, everyone is glad to be here. Look at all the smiles and fellowship. It's a sight to see, *jah*?"

"It is, indeed."

"It's a blessing to get together for a good cause, May. Everyone knows your family is grateful, but you ain't the only person who feels lifted."

May smiled again before continuing around the tables and offering drinks to the men. Daniel was correct. While there were a few men who simply held out their hand for a refill, most thanked her politely and poured their own, after waving off her thanks.

When the lemonade pitcher was empty, she walked over to the large container and filled it again. She smiled when she realized that the next man she was offering a drink to was Carl. He'd taken his baseball cap off his head and placed it on his lap. "Hiya. Would you care for something more to drink?"

"I would," he said as he took the pitcher out of her hands. "How are you holding up?"

"I am fine. Excited that a new barn is taking shape so quickly. How are you holding up?" When confusion played across his features, Camille's words rang in her head. Quickly, she made sure to clarify her words so he wouldn't think that she was referring to his physical well-being. "Is it strange being one of just a handful of Englishers on the work crew?"

"Not for me, but I have gotten my share of ribbing. It's all in fun."

"We've been teasing each other all day, May," Bradley Mahlon explained. "If it weren't about Carl being English, it would be about something else."

Carl lowered his voice. "Don't worry about me, May. I can hold my own."

"I'm sure you can," she said softly. Feeling Bradley's interest on the two of them, May inclined her head. "Thank you both for being here." The formal thanks felt a bit foolish to say to Carl.

His expression warmed. "It's a wonderful day, May. Ain't so?"

"The best."

"I'll come find you toward sunset. Maybe we could sit together when we have supper?"

"I'd like that."

He put his ball cap on his head, the brim turned toward his back as he seemed to like to do. "*Gut.*"

His expression—and his warm promise—kept her spirits uplifted through the next four hours. Daniel had been right. Though the women were not scaling barns, cutting wood, or hammering nails, they were working just as hard. They'd cleaned up the luncheon, organized children and the new women who arrived, and then began preparations for supper, which included hot dogs and hamburgers, baked beans, coleslaw, bean salad, watermelon, and a variety of sheet cakes. A couple of ladies had donated their canned relishes and chutney.

They all worked to arrange the condiments, onions, tomatoes, and lettuce on plates as well.

At sunset, most of the barn had been completed. Over the next week, Walker, her father, and several of the best carpenters in Apple Creek would put the finishing touches on the structure. But what mattered the most to their family was that they'd have a safe place for their herd of alpacas to sleep at night. No longer would they have to keep watch for coyotes.

Because some people were going home, while others intended to stay for a while after supper and enjoy each other's company, the women had elected not to serve another big meal.

Instead, everything was set up in four buffet lines. Two teenagers were assigned to each line to refill bowls as needed. May's mother had at first worried that everyone might feel disappointed, but the other women had persuaded her to listen to their advice.

The ladies had been right, too. Everyone seemed relaxed and happy as they slowly made their way through the lines, then dined picnic-style in various spots around the Schotts' farm.

She found Carl waiting for her next to the line for the buffet. Most of the older men and women were near the front, with the youngest members of the gathering near the end of the line. Everyone was chatting animatedly, though several called out to see if she wanted to join them.

"*Danke*, but I have plans," she explained.

"She's with me," Carl said with a grin. Lowering his voice, he said, "I'm glad you're here. I was about to go looking for you."

"What? Are you hungry again?" she teased.

"I can't believe it, but I'm near starving. I heard we're having a barbecue. Is that true?"

"*Jah*. When *mei mamm* started worrying about how we'd prepare so much chicken, Lovina took over. Next thing we knew, she'd gathered some of the older men and put them on grilling duty. They've been having a good time, and the women are very glad not to be attempting to prepare chicken casseroles for a hundred people."

"Gestures like that make me miss living Amish. I've never met a group of people so able to work easily together, whether it's for a gathering planned for six months or a barn raising planned in just a week."

May felt the same way. "My family's been blessed twice to host two barn raisings. I don't know if we could've survived without everyone's help."

To her surprise, Carl's expression warmed. "You are amazing, May. Most people would be focusing on the fact that you've lost your barn twice. Once through a fire caused by lightning and once because of a tornado. But here you are, actually telling me that you are blessed."

She looked away. "The help has been a blessing. I . . . I still regret luring you into the barn in the first place."

"May, look at me. I'm not a follower. I'm not weakminded. Not now, and not when I was a teenager. I wanted to go there with you." Not seeming to care that their conversation was undoubtedly being watched by at least a couple of dozen people, Carl moved closer and spoke into her ear. "I wanted to kiss you, May. I went in that barn of my own free will. You didn't coerce me into anything I didn't want to do. Do you understand?"

Breathless, she nodded.

Still disregarding everyone else, he pressed on. "Are you sure? Because I don't want you to worry about being at fault ever again."

"I'm sure." And yes, her voice did sound rather thready.

"*Gut.*" He grinned. "Now come do what you promised and join me in line. We'll get our supper and sit together and chat. You can even whisper to me who these men are so I don't offend them by not remembering."

"I can't wait. Come along, Carl," she teased as she led the way to the end of the line. They might still have unresolved issues between them, but their actions six years ago were no longer one of them.

Now all they had to figure out was what to do about their future. He hadn't asked her yet, but eventually she needed to decide if she was willing to give him up . . . or leave Apple Creek—and live English by his side.

Chapter 37

Carl was sitting in the back of Bruno's for another conference call. Since it was in the middle of the afternoon, after lunch but hours before dinner, Bruno didn't mind if he sat at a table for a spell, sipping iced tea and enjoying a bowl of minestrone soup.

As usual, the conference call felt long, but there was an underlying tension coming from his boss that Carl couldn't quite place. For the last five minutes, he'd been wracking his brain, wondering what he'd done wrong with one of the projects he'd just completed.

Finally, after the other two sales associates got off, his manager said, "Would you stay on the line a moment?"

"Of course. Is everything all right?"

"Everything is good. We're all happy with your performance, too."

"I'm glad . . ."

"Here's the deal. We really need you back in the office, Carl," Whit said. "As much as I commend you for returning to your roots and reconnecting with your family, we need you closer."

Though Whit's statement wasn't a surprise, it took the wind out of Carl's sails. "I understand."

"Do you? I talked to Jerry. He's concerned that you might be wanting to leave the company. Is that the case, Carl? Are you unhappy here?"

He closed his eyes. "*Nee*. I mean, no," he said quickly. "I'm happy with Convergent and want to continue." That was true, too. He had a good job and made a good living. In addition, both Whit and Jerry were good men to work for. They were fair and supportive. Whit, especially, had helped him learn a lot about being a good salesman, especially during his first year, when he'd been unsure and tentative about just about everything.

"I'm really glad to hear you say that. Really glad."

"When would you like me there full-time?"

"As soon as possible."

It was Thursday. "Like, Monday?"

"Can you be here then?"

Could he do that? Yes, he could. Did he want to go back to the city on Monday? Not particularly. Inwardly, he sighed. He'd known this day would be coming, and he'd planned on it, too. He'd even made a special purchase in preparation for it. "Yes."

"Great. I'll pass on the word. Hey, take tomorrow off, okay? I'm sure you're going to want to spend another day with your family before you drive back."

"Thank you."

"You're welcome. See you Monday. Have a good weekend."

"Thanks, Whit. You, too."

When he put down his cell phone, his insides were churning. His visit to Apple Creek was over.

As he drove home, he realized that the things he'd accomplished had nothing to do with what he'd planned to achieve. He'd returned to Apple Creek with the intention of coming to terms with his scars and finally facing May and her family.

He'd envisioned that there would be a lot of hurt feelings, anger, and maybe even the realization that it wasn't possible to go back to the way things used to be.

He'd returned for closure.

Instead, the opposite had happened. He'd discovered that the people who cared about him didn't care about his scars. Oh, they felt sorry for him and had worried about the pain he'd undergone over the years, but his outward appearance hadn't spurred much conversation at all.

Instead, they quickly reminded him that all that mattered was the person he was inside. As far as everyone else was concerned, he was still Carl Hilty, Robin and Able's eldest.

Recalling the way Kevin, Ally, and his parents had inspected him with his shirt off, Carl realized that they hadn't been cautious or bashful about examining him. They looked for positives, too. They looked for healing instead of damage.

It was a much healthier way to see things, he decided as he parked his truck and walked into the farmhouse.

His visit had brought a great many blessings and things to celebrate.

The only question was how to tell May.

"Brother, you look like you've got the weight of the world on your shoulders," Ally said as she came in from working in the vegetable garden. "What happened?"

"My boss said they need me back in the office."

"When?"

"Monday."

Her eyes widened. "That's soon."

"It is." He pushed his dismay to one side. He was an adult with a good job. He had responsibilities, too. "I was hoping I'd be able to stay here longer, but I guess that was too much to ask for. I have a good job at Convergent, and I need to be involved." Thinking about how few hours he'd been working in comparison to his usual schedule made him wince. His managers really had been more than patient with him. "I'm grateful that I could stay this long."

"I'm grateful for your visit, too, especially since, you know, we almost lost everything when a tornado hit our farm."

He chuckled. "You're exactly right."

"Now that I'm married, you should listen to me more."

"Oh, brother. I hope when Walker realizes just how full of yourself you are, he doesn't have regrets about being hitched to you for the rest of his life."

"I promise, he thinks I'm worth it." She smiled, looking completely content.

"I'm happy for ya."

"*Danke*. Now, try not to fret too much—or let Mamm and Daed make you feel guilty about your responsibilities here. We'll just have to make plans for you to return when you can. Maybe on Independence Day."

"*Jah*. That's only about six weeks away. Not too far at all."

Her expression softened. "For some reason, I don't think you're dreading going back to work on Monday. That's not what's bothering you, is it?"

He couldn't deny the truth. "It isn't. I like my job. It's leaving here that will be difficult. Ally, I hadn't expected to feel so comfortable here. I guess I assumed that after living among the English for so long, I wouldn't ever want to live in an Amish house."

"Maybe it wasn't the Amish way of life that made you feel comfortable as much as being around your family."

He nodded. "*Jah*. That . . . that is correct."

"We'll still be here, Carl. We were here all this time."

"I know." He swallowed, wanting to convey his feelings clearly. "I was always available for you, too. I'm sorry if you thought that you had to deal with everything on your own."

"I didn't, though I would be lying if I didn't admit that

dealing with the Schott family became easier with you here."
She tilted her head to one side. "Of course, now you have to
figure out what to do about May."

There wasn't anything to figure out. Carl knew without a
doubt that he wanted May in his life. He'd even taken the
first step toward fulfilling that dream. What he did need to
learn was whether she felt the same way—and if she was
willing to make the change to live as an Englisher.

"I think I need to go talk to her about everything."

"You sure do."

"What am I going to do if she says that she doesn't want
to move? Do I quit my job and stay here?"

"Somehow, I don't think it's as easy as that. You've already made the choice, ain't so? I reckon even Preacher Elias
would say that one can't move in and out of our way of
life—or our faith—as it suits one. You probably also can't
try to make yourself fit into a way of life that you've left behind. What would happen to your relationship with May if
you did that?"

The thought brought him up short. If he tried to become
something he wasn't, then he wouldn't be the same man.

"May told me that she liked the man I am now."

"Then you need to trust that, right?"

He nodded. "Right."

She waved her hands. "I think you should go talk to her."
Looking mischievous, she added, "Why don't you take the
buggy?"

"In my jeans, T-shirt, and baseball cap?"

"I don't think Gingersnap is going to care what you're
wearing, Carl. The question is whether or not you can still
drive a buggy."

"I'm going to take the courting buggy."

"That's a great choice. Now, go before Mamm and Daed
get involved and you have another two-hour conversation
about your life."

That warning was enough to spur him into action. "I'll see ya later."

"Use the light tan leather bridle. That's Gingersnap's favorite."

"*Danke.*" After hurrying to his room to make some quick preparations, he strode to the barn. He was actually glad he was going to go calling on May in a buggy instead of his truck. There was something fitting about straddling both worlds while planning a future with her.

He only hoped that May would feel the same way.

Chapter 38

May had just gotten Prancer, Dasher, and Donner's attention for another enrichment activity when the buggy rolled
up the drive.

Like the curious alpacas they were, the three suddenly ignored her treats and trotted over to the fence line to get a
better look at the new arrival.

May was annoyed by the interruption—until she turned
to get a better look at the new arrival herself. She couldn't
deny that the sight was worth staring at. After all, it wasn't
every day that one watched the arrival of an Englisher ex-
pertly driving an Amish courting buggy!

She leaned her elbows on the fence and watched Carl approach. To her amusement, the three two-year-old alpacas
stood on either side of her, practically spellbound.

When Dasher moved his ears forward and tilted his head
to one side, she giggled. "The sight is very curious, for sure
and for certain, Dash. But in all the best ways, right?"

Dasher hummed in response.

After looking a little confused before he set the parking

brake and hopped out, Carl turned her way with a confident stride.

It was obvious that he had noticed her right away, too.

"What are you doing, Carl?" she called out when he got close. "Making sure you can still drive a buggy?"

"I knew I could." He chuckled. "Gingersnap wasn't too sure of it, though. He could tell that my hands weren't as firm on the reins as they should've been." He stopped in front of May. "I must say that you make almost as good a picture here as I do on the courting buggy. What are you doing?"

"I'm doing enrichment with the two-year-old boys." She pushed her clicker to demonstrate. "We're working on lying down on command."

"How's that going?"

"Obviously, not so well." She laughed. "They like the attention and having to concentrate, though, so it's all worth it. A bored alpaca is a dangerous one."

"I'll take your word for it."

"That's smart. Trust me, you don't want to speak from personal experience." When he smiled at her again, she asked, "Is there a reason you came over?"

"Obviously, I came over to take you on a buggy ride."

"In the middle of a Thursday?"

"Is there something wrong with going for a ride on a Thursday afternoon?"

She was making a cake of herself. "Of course not."

"Are you too busy to go out? Does your mother need you to cook or something?"

"*Nee*. I helped her prepare a casserole this morning."

He raised an eyebrow. "So . . ."

"You're right. Let me bring these guys inside, and then I'll tell Mamm what I'm doing."

"How can I help?" Carl asked.

"Wait for me?"

"Of course, I can do that."

May felt her cheeks flush as she realized that she really was smitten with everything about Carl. "I'll be right back."

"No need to hurry, May. I came over here for you, ya know. I don't mind waiting."

His words were kind, but they hit her hard; everything he was saying felt like a promise of so much more. Which was foolish. She was no longer sixteen to his seventeen. Hadn't she gotten more calm and collected since then? It seemed she hadn't at all.

Feeling frustrated with herself, May signaled for Prancer, Dasher, and Donner to follow her into the barn. At first, the trio didn't pay her much mind at all. Honestly, it seemed that they were far more excited to see Carl than to pay attention to her.

She knew the feeling.

"Sorry, gentlemen, but Carl ain't here for you. He's come to see me, so you need to go into the barn."

The alpacas looked at each other for a full minute.

She tapped her foot. "Now, if you please."

At last, Prancer followed her, which made the others get into line right behind him.

After giving them some treats, she hurried out of the barn. Carl was now speaking to Walker. Relieved that he wasn't standing there impatiently waiting, she strode into the house.

Her mother was in the kitchen. She looked relieved when May entered. "Oh, good. I was wondering when you were gonna come back inside. I need your help. Ally and Walker are joining us for supper tonight." Pointing to a basket of freshly picked beans, she added, "Get to work on the string beans. I need to put them in the pot soon."

"I'm sorry, but I can't, Mamm. Carl is here."

"He is? Well, that is nice. He can stay for supper; we'll have plenty." She looked around. "Where is he?"

"He's outside talking to Walker."

She frowned. "Oh no. Did something happen?" She worried her bottom lip. "I hope it doesn't involve Ally. Hasn't she seemed more lighthearted of late?"

"I don't think anything is wrong with anyone. Carl's here to take me on a buggy ride."

Her mother chuckled. "Is that what he's started calling rides in his big truck now?"

"*Nee*, Mamm. He really did drive a buggy over. Gingersnap is out there and everything."

Looking completely confused, her mother peered out the kitchen window. "I don't see him. Did he decide to join the church after all? Wait, he drove over a courting buggy."

She couldn't contain her smile. "I know."

"May, what's going on?"

"I . . . I'm not really sure. I was with the alpacas when he arrived, so we haven't really talked. I need to go change. I only came in to tell you that I'm going out with him for a while." And . . . she needed to do that right away. "I'd better hurry."

"But what about supper?"

"Don't worry about supper for me," she said as she headed toward the stairs.

To her dismay, her mother followed on her heels. "Hold on, May. Maybe we should talk about things."

"I don't think so. I need to get dressed."

"But—"

"Mamm, I'm serious. Everything is good." She trotted up the rest of the stairs and walked into her room, closing the door behind her. Opening up her wardrobe, she saw her new dress. It was a deep raspberry color. The fabric was a bit nicer than her usual choice. It was softer and seemed to glide over her body. It also had short sleeves. She'd never worn it. She'd been telling herself that she was going to save it for

Easter, but it had been rainy and cold, so she'd worn a long-sleeved blue dress then.

This dress had been waiting for her for months now, just waiting for the perfect occasion. Today was the day.

After unpinning her work dress, taking it off, washing her hands and face, and donning and pinning her fresh dress, May was starting to feel that she was woefully late. She hoped Carl had been speaking the truth when he'd said that he didn't mind waiting for her. After slipping her feet into new pink Keds, she grabbed her purse and ran back downstairs.

There was Carl again, standing in the foyer, chatting with her mother.

"I'm ready," she called out.

He immediately turned to look up at her. And then he smiled. "Look at you."

"I . . . I was a mess after working with the alpacas all afternoon. I wanted to get cleaned up." Uh oh. Was that too much information?

"You look pretty."

"*Danke.*" She glanced at her mother, silently begging her not to say a word. Her prayers must have been answered because her mother only smiled and folded her hands at her waist.

"Are you ready?"

"*Jah.*" She smiled up at Carl as he opened the door and escorted her out.

"So I guess you've noticed the buggy."

"I did. And Gingersnap."

He stuffed his hands in his jeans' pockets. "Is this all right with you?"

Carl looked so tentative and sweet. It was adorable and unexpected. He was acting almost like a suitor.

No, exactly like a suitor.

"I think it's perfect. I haven't been on a buggy ride in a long time."

"What do you mean?"

Carl looked completely confused, and why wouldn't he be? She was Amish. Her family had a buggy and a buggy horse at her house. Of course, she went on buggy rides—and drove a buggy—all the time.

"I mean, I haven't been in a courting buggy for a while. Um, you know, like this."

"Like this."

"*Jah*." She bit her lip. Why had she said that? Carl was either going to think that no man had ever taken an interest in her—or that she was making him into some kind of ardent suitor.

Carl seemed to weigh her statement for a moment, then nodded. "Good." He murmured something to Gingersnap and clicked his tongue. When the horse sped up a bit, he smiled.

She laughed. "You are enjoying this, aren't you?"

"Very much."

His pleased expression made everything seem just fine again. No, better than fine. This moment wasn't exactly like her teenaged dreams of falling in love. It was better.

What mattered was that she had finally started doing things for herself. Instead of simply dreaming about fairy tales, she was living her dreams, one day at a time.

Chapter 39

It turned out that driving a buggy was a lot like riding a bike. He might be a little rusty, but so far he was doing okay. Gingersnap hadn't balked yet, which was a blessing.

So the actual buggy ride was good. However, as far as the date went . . . he wasn't exactly sure. May had been pretty quiet after admitting that she hadn't been on a lot of dates— at least not the courting buggy kind.

He didn't know if May was embarrassed about sharing that information or perhaps feeling slighted because he hadn't reciprocated with any of his dating stories. As Gingersnap clip-clopped along, he weighed both reasons and came up short.

What did it even matter? It wasn't as if he was going to start hammering her with questions.

"Um, what are you doing, Carl?"

"I thought we already talked about me driving the buggy." Realizing that he sounded defensive, he mentally winced. Smooth, he was not.

Her eyes sparkled as she shook her head. "I'm sorry, but I

still don't really get why you didn't drive your truck. As far as I've been able to tell, you drive that just fine, and I don't mind riding in it either. Why did you decide to hitch up a buggy for today's outing?"

Gingersnap whickered as if to say he was curious to know, too.

Though he wasn't thrilled with the horse's cheeky attitude, he couldn't blame the gelding—or May's confusion. It was time to start talking and hope at least some of his words made a lick of sense.

"We've driven around in my truck a lot, so I thought it might be fun to do something different." He'd actually thought it would be more romantic.

"Oh. Well, yes . . . I suppose it is."

Faint praise, indeed. Carl supposed it was time he dug a little deeper and gave her a better explanation. "May, I guess I wanted to do something that was familiar to you instead of constantly reminding us both that I'm no longer Amish and you are."

She frowned. "Why?"

Why? "I don't know. Maybe I've also been trying to remind myself that I might have a different life up in Cleveland, but I'm not a completely different person than I used to be."

At last, some of the worry that had been shining in her eyes eased. "That makes sense."

At least it did to her. Almost reluctantly, the horse continued to meander down the narrow road. No cars were passing them, and the air was comfortable and smelled so good—like fresh grass, wildflowers, and home. Next to him, May sat quiet and composed—and looked so pretty. She had on an unfamiliar dark pink dress, matching apron . . . and pink Keds tennis shoes. Her hands were neatly folded in her lap.

His outfit of jeans, T-shirt, tennis shoes, and ball cap seemed shabby in comparison. He really should have at least put on a collared shirt.

Gingersnap continued down the road, then turned right, heading down the Holsts' lane almost of her own accord.

Noticing that May was looking around eagerly, obviously curious to see what their destination was, Carl realized he wasn't just underdressed, he was unprepared. He didn't have a blanket or a picnic basket. Actually, beyond the ring he'd picked out earlier that week, he had nothing quaint or romantic or special that would let May know how much this outing meant to him.

How could he have been so thoughtless? He had a sister. He was friends with several women at work who shared stories with him about their husbands and their daughters. He knew that women liked men to put some thought and effort into special occasions. He'd known that—and yet, here he was, pretending to guide a horse who was actually taking him down an unfamiliar road.

He was pretty certain that by the time he actually got down on one knee and proposed, May was either going to burst out laughing or demand to be taken home immediately.

Disgusted with himself, he pulled on Gingersnap's reins. The horse stopped but pawed at the ground.

Yep, it was a fact. Even the horse knew he was messing everything up.

"Carl? What's wrong? Why did you stop?"

He swallowed and tried to sound normal and not like the nervous wreck he was. "It, ah, just occurred to me that I have no idea where to take you. I've been pretty much following Gingersnap's lead."

She giggled. "Ally has always said that he is the smartest horse in Apple Creek. I never believed her until now."

"Does that mean I haven't gotten us lost?"

"You haven't gotten us lost at all, Carl. As you know, we're on the edge of the Holsts' land. There's a nice pond on it. Ally and *mei bruder* go there quite a bit." Looking a little embarrassed, she added, "I mean, they did until they got married."

"Should we continue there? Or is there someplace else you'd rather go?"

"As I told you, I haven't been on too many buggy outings. Not with beaus, and not even with my family. My parents never have been the type to want to drive around for no reason."

"I'm surprised."

"Why?"

"You're so pretty." Plus, she was May. He'd always found everything about her to be special. "And you're sweet, too."

"*Danke.* I have been courted a little bit, but I wasn't interested in any of those men." She looked as if she was about to add something but refrained.

"I'm glad." He guided Gingersnap to the right. "I don't remember there being much traffic on this lane. Is that okay?"

"Of course."

He made sure to keep to the side so vehicles could pass. A passenger van did, then a truck, then it was thankfully quiet. Since May seemed to be content to simply sit by his side, he eventually began to focus on the clip-clop of Gingersnap's hooves, the birds calling out to each other, the low hum of crickets . . . the faint buzz of a tractor in the distance.

"The road veers to the right up here. It's kind of sharp," May warned.

Carl was just about to pull on the reins to slow the horse, but Gingersnap seemed to be more familiar with the lane than he was. She slowed down and was already turning before he did a thing.

As they continued, rows of corn rose up on either side of them. But instead of feeling suffocating, the tall rows felt comforting, as if they were providing privacy from the outside world. Of course, that was how all of Apple Creek was—familiar and comfortable. Peaceful.

Up ahead was the Holsts' pond. When they neared, Carl set the brake in a grassy spot. Then he helped May out and finally unhitched Gingersnap so he could enjoy the warm day and fresh grass as much as they did.

Finally, he reached for her hand. They walked to the bank of the pond. Cattails had sprung up nearby. Flowers and green shrubs and bushes surrounded the far bank. "This is really nice, May."

"I love it here."

"I'm afraid I'm hopelessly unprepared. I should've brought a quilt or a blanket for us to sit on and a picnic basket or something so you could have a snack and a drink."

"There is a nice log right here—that's good enough for me, Carl. And I'm not hungry or thirsty." She sat down and kicked her legs out, the pink canvas tennis shoes making him smile.

He sat down next to her. The movement made the log shift a bit.

"Oh!" May grabbed hold of his arm.

He chuckled. "I've got you, May." When she gazed up at him and smiled, he felt his heart quicken a bit. She really was so pretty.

"What?"

"Nothing. I, uh, I was just thinking I'd almost forgotten how beautiful it is out here."

"I guess it is different from your place in Cleveland."

He lived in a two-bedroom condo within walking distance of a lot of restaurants and shops. Instead of birdsong, there was always a low buzz of traffic in the air. "You could say that," he said lightly.

"What do you do for fun? Do you go to movies and such?"

"A lot of people do; not me, though." Thinking about his usual weekends—he generally slept late, watched television, and ran errands; he frowned. Then he remembered something he'd done just a couple of days before deciding to come to Apple Creek for a spell. "The other day, I drove to Lake Erie. Sometimes I park and walk on the paths near the water. In the winter, much of it is covered by ice and snow, and geese and other birds rest on it. In the spring and summer, though, it's glorious. Once a year, I visit a bay and go canoeing." At her questioning look, he added, "There are lots of those near Lake Erie. Have you been?"

"To Lake Erie? *Nee.*"

"I'm surprised, but that's good news for me. I'd like to take you there one day."

May looked wistful. "I'd like that."

"I'd like to show you. Maybe we'll even go on one of those tours. You can board a ship where they play music, and you get to visit various islands. It's fun."

"It sounds fun. You know, I almost went, once," she said after a pause.

"Really? What stopped you?"

"You. After the fire, I didn't want to have fun anymore. I wanted to see you so badly, but when I called, you asked me not to come."

Carl remembered their conversation after Walker proposed to Ally, when May had tried to talk to him about that time. "I wasn't in a good place back then."

She laughed softly. "You said the same thing to me when we talked a few weeks ago, and it sounds just as condescending as it did then. Don't you think I know the hospital wasn't a good place?"

She'd taken his words literally. "You misunderstood what I meant. I meant I wasn't in a good place." He waved a hand.

"You know, mentally. I was in a lot of pain—and on a lot of medicine because of that pain. I could hardly get through each day." As much as he hated to recall it, he added, "There were some days when I could barely get through each hour. I wouldn't even let my family see me."

More worry entered her eyes. "That's why your mother wasn't living in Cleveland with you?"

He nodded. "I asked her to leave after two weeks. Kevin and Ally were still young, Daed had the farm, and there wasn't much for Mamm to do besides watch me and try to not cry." Though he hated revealing his weakness, he forced himself to continue. May deserved to know the truth. "It was exhausting trying to pretend to be okay when I felt like I was anything but that."

Her brown eyes looked even more troubled. "I had no idea things were that bad for that long."

"Why would you?"

She placed a hand on his arm. "*Nee*, Carl. The question isn't why would I know but rather why didn't I know? You were everything to me. I should've known."

"There wasn't anything you could do, May."

"Maybe I didn't need to solve your problems as much as I wanted to simply be let in on them. We were close, Carl. Really close."

"You're right. We were." Her words made sense. They made sense and made him wonder if things would have been different if he'd been willing to let her in. "I'd say I was sorry for keeping you out, but I don't know if I could've been any different."

"I don't think there's anything we can say that will change the past."

"You're right. There's nothing to be gained by rehashing it." He leaned back on his hands. "I think it's better to simply enjoy days like today. Ain't so?"

"Always. It's a lovely day, and we're together. I'll make

sure to keep this memory close in my heart when you're back in Cleveland."

There it was. His opening. "Actually, I wanted to talk to you about that. I need to go back soon."

"How soon?"

"Monday."

Her eyes widened. "I'll miss you."

"I'll miss you, too." He shook his head, once again frustrated with himself. "But, um, thinking about the future and all . . ."

"Yes?"

"I thought that maybe we should talk about it."

"What about?"

Lord, please help me, he silently prayed. *Please help me stop making such a mess of this.* "Well, um, there's probably lots for us to discuss. For example, have you decided about getting baptized yet?"

May's eyes widened before she pulled herself together again. "I think I have."

"What are you thinking? I mean, what have you decided to do?"

She looked down at her pink dress. Smoothed out a wrinkle. "I'm leaning toward not becoming Amish."

A burst of happiness ran through him. "Why?"

"A number of reasons." She waited a beat, then added, "I'm just going to be honest, Carl. I . . . well, I, well, even after all this time, I still have feelings for you."

He shifted so he could take her hands. Rubbing a thumb along the knuckles of her left hand, he whispered, "You do, huh?"

Twin patches of pink dotted her cheeks. "I do. Have I just embarrassed both of us?"

"*Nee.* You've made me very happy. May, you always were the bravest girl I knew. Here I am, biding my time, trying to get the courage to tell you about my feelings for you and failing miserably. And you just went right ahead."

Humor lit her eyes. "Are you saying that I stole your thunder?"

"No, I'm saying that I obviously need you in my life all the time." He leaned close and kissed her cheek. "May, you've just made me so happy. I still have feelings for you, too." No, he wasn't going to do this. He wasn't going to do things halfway. "I don't just 'have feelings' for you, May Schott. I love you. I love you so much."

May's lips were slightly parted as she stared at him in obvious wonder. "Carl?"

"I've loved you since we were small. I loved you when we went into your barn during the storm. I loved you when I was covered in bandages and didn't want you to see me be a person I couldn't be proud of . . ."

"And now?"

"Now I love you as a grown man who understands what I lost and appreciates what I can have—if I dare to make my dream come true."

She blinked. "Carl—"

"No, listen, hear me out. I know I'm not much to look at anymore, but I think the Lord made allowances for that. What he took from me in looks, he gave back to me in other ways. I'm smarter than I used to be, May. My edges are smoother. My heart is bigger. I won't hurt yours, May. I promise, I'll take care of it and work hard to make sure you don't regret trusting me with it."

She squeezed his hand. Hard. "Carl!"

"Yes?"

She chuckled. "You are a handful, Carl Hilty. You wear a ball cap and jeans to drive a courting buggy. You bare your soul to me and don't give a girl a chance to make amends or even try to make you feel better. You just plow through like a workhorse."

"I need guidance, I really do."

"Yes, you do. You're in luck, though, because I am right here."

This was the moment. At last. Releasing her hands, he knelt down on the ground in front of her. Pulled out the ring in a box he'd wrapped and tied with a white satin ribbon. "May, I . . . I've been thinking about this moment for quite some time. I wanted to do this right, and because I'm English now, I wanted to give you a proper ring." He carefully unwrapped the ring and held it out to her. "Would you consider always being by my side? Will you wear my ring and let me love you? Will you marry me, at long last?"

She stared at the ring. Looked up into his eyes, and then smiled so sweetly. "Yes, Carl. I will marry you." She held out her left hand.

It was trembling. It was likely as shaky as his own. Still afraid that he was going to drop it, he carefully slipped the ring on her finger. The thin gold band with the small round diamond looked perfect.

Unable to help himself, he lifted her hand and kissed it. "I'll make you happy, May. I promise."

"I know you will."

Carefully framing her face in his hands, he kissed her at last. Kissed her with as much passion and longing as he'd felt all those years ago. Maybe even more so now, because he knew what his life was like without her. He knew what he'd almost lost.

May wrapped her arms around his waist and held on tight, answering each one of his kisses with another of her own.

When he pulled away at last, Carl smiled. "I can't believe you said yes so easily."

"I can't believe you waited so long."

He couldn't believe it either. They'd waited so long, but perhaps it had been just long enough. Perhaps they'd needed time to grow up, time to heal, time to remember what was important and what wasn't.

Perhaps the Lord really was patient and kind and forgiving. And maybe He answered prayers, too.

Pulling her closer, he kissed her again. This time, May met him halfway, wrapped her arms around his neck and held on tight.

Giving him everything he desired and more than he ever dreamed of having.

When they finally broke apart, her sweet laughter floated through the air, drifting over the fields surrounding them.

Startling Gingersnap, who'd been happily munching on fresh grass the whole time. She blew out air, sounding annoyed.

"Sorry, but you're just going to have to wait a bit for us, Gingersnap," he murmured. "This is a pretty important moment for me and May. We'll be on our way in a little while."

May tilted her head. "Are you ready to leave? So soon?"

"Not at all. But I wouldn't mind eventually driving my fiancée around for a bit. It is a courting buggy, you know. I'd hate to put it to waste."

May laughed again as he pulled her back into his arms and held her close. She felt good and special and right. Sitting there, on the side of a pond with cattails and fresh flowers and an annoyed horse nearby, Carl reckoned no moment could ever be better. Far better than he used to imagine it might be, once so very long ago.

Once upon a time, when they were young and impetuous and so full of dreams.

Read on for a special preview of Shelley Shepard Gray's
next heartwarming novel . . .

AN AMISH CINDERELLA

**In this sweet, heartfelt novel set in the charming close-knit
Amish community of Apple Creek, Ohio, it's going to take
a prince among men to woo this hardworking young
woman away from her misgivings about love . . .**

Now that her friends are all marrying or moving away, Heart
Beachy has started feeling lonely. Worse, everyone keeps
asking when she's going to find a man of her own. Don't they
realize Heart has her hands full at home with her widowed
dad, too many chores, and a menagerie of needy, small
animals? Besides, she doesn't understand the fuss about
marriage. It's enough to make her consider finally becoming a
pet-sitter, or moving to an *English* community, where she
won't be an oddity . . .

Newcomer Clayton Glick is utterly charmed by Heart—and
completely confounded. He can't figure out why this beautiful
woman is as awkward as a teenager whenever he's around,
which is often now that he's an apprentice to her blacksmith
father. So Clayton starts assisting with Heart's never-ending
tasks, even helping her corral her unruly pets. How else can
he court an adorably flustered woman who doesn't know the
first thing about courtship? Because courting is exactly what
he intends . . .

Heart doesn't know why her pulse hammers every time she
sees Clayton. She only knows yielding to such emotions will
mean trouble. . . . But maybe with a little faith—and the trying
on of a shoe—Clayton can convince her to join him on the
road to happily ever after.

Coming soon from Kensington Publishing Corp.

Chapter 1

September

Right outside of the kitchen window, the first leaves on the Aspen trees her grandfather had planted were starting to turn. Haphazardly spaced gold leaves now dotted each one, decorating each like precious jewels. Mums were taking shape, and the hedge of burning bushes were slowly turning red, and the early morning air was crisp and cool. Silly squirrels and chipmunks darted here and there, industriously gathering acorns and pine needles for their nests. Fall was coming on fast.

Soon, everyone in Apple Creek would be looking forward to attending the annual fall festival or picking pumpkins or venturing over to other towns to take part in their corn mazes.

Just like in years past.

Heart Beachy pressed a hand to the glass pane and dreamed about doing such things. If she had an outing planned with a handsome suitor, she'd make a new dress for it. Perhaps something in a shade of cranberry. Her mother used to say that shades of red complemented Heart's blue eyes and blond hair nicely.

"Nee, Mamm didn't say that," Heart said out loud. Turning her voice an octave higher, she mimicked, "Hazel, I do like you in red. It sets off your *beautiful* blue eyes."

Remembering how much she'd love to hear her mother's sweet words, Heart smiled. Her mother always had encouraging words of praise for her only child.

On the heels of that good memory was a far less appealing one. Instead of hugging her mamm for making her feel special and good, all she'd ever done was scowl and state that she hated her name and wanted to be called "Heart" instead.

Though her words had been true-after all, who really wanted to be named Hazel?-Heart felt her insides cringe. She'd been such a spoiled child. Such a willful little girl. It was no wonder that at least two afternoons a week Mamm would send Heart out to go "help" her daed in his blacksmith workshop.

The barn had been hot and filled with dangerous things, but her father had never seemed to mind her being with him. He'd given her a little chair in the corner and small tasks to do.

With a sigh, she turned away from the kitchen window. If she had just one more day with her mother, she'd be so happy. She'd tell her just how much she loved her. How grateful she was to have such a sweet and loving mamm.

But, of course, wishes and dreams were for other folks. It seemed that so much of what she'd asked for never were going to come true. For some reason, maybe the Lord had decided that she had enough.

The back door opened with a rough clack. "Heart, you have dinner on the table yet?"

She felt like pointing to the kitchen clock above the door. She served her father's midday meal at eleven every day. Always. Daed had come in early. "Not yet. I'll have it out soon."

"When?"

She rolled her eyes. "In seven minutes, Daed. When it's eleven."

He scowled. "It ain't ready early?"

"It is not." When her father looked ready to complain, she said, "Hold your horses."

"Fine. I'm gonna wash up."

Even from the kitchen she could hear him stomp to the sink, just off the hallway.

Her father still had on his boots-he never did listen to her when she explained how dirty they got her freshly swept floor. He'd always look mystified about why that was a concern of hers.

Knowing that some things would never change, she pulled out a bowl and silverware. Then decided to switch things up a bit. Maybe for once she'd wait to eat until later. Maybe after she went for a walk or something.

Carefully she spooned a hearty portion of shepherd's pie into his bowl. Ground beef mixed with fresh vegetables, potatoes and gravy. The top layer of mashed potatoes was golden brown.

She'd just placed it on the table when her father returned. "Ah, Heart. You do have a way with meat and potatoes."

This was high praise from her father, but as compliments went, there was a lot to be desired. "*Danke.*"

Sitting down, he looked at the empty space in front of her. "Where is your food?"

"I decided to wait to eat."

"Why?"

"I'm not too hungry. Besides it's a pretty fall day. I was thinking that I might go on a walk."

After her father bowed his head in silent prayer, he dug in.

Several minutes passed before he responded. "Where are you going to walk to?"

"I'm not sure."

"You planning on visiting some of the neighbors?"

"Maybe."

"Mary Miller ain't far. Maybe you could check on her. She's got puppies, I heard."

"I'll definitely have to go see them. Did her Golden have the litter?"

He nodded. "Since you've been thinking about one day pet-sitting you ought to lend her a hand." He took another bite. "If you have time, that is."

"I can make time to help Mary. Danke, Daed."

"Just be home by three o'clock."

"Why?"

"Someone's coming over who I want you to meet."

This conversation was getting curiouser and curiouser. Her father did blacksmithing and ironworks for lots of people, but none of them were of much interest to Heart. "Who?"

"You'll see. Just be home by three." Looking around the kitchen, he added, "And maybe you could make some of your cereal treats?"

He sounded so hopeful, she hid a smile. Her father might be several inches over six feet and built like a linebacker on a football team, but he had a soft spot for Rice Krispies Treats. He had no idea that making them took no time at all.

"Jah, Daed. I'll be glad to make those."

"Gut." He scooted out his chair and strode to the door. It slammed behind him. Leaving behind a trail of dirt.

The right thing to do would be to eat her meal, sweep the floor, make the cereal treats, and wash all the dishes. But she'd had enough. She needed a break.

Instead, she covered the pie with some waxed paper, set it

in the fridge, and walked out the door. She might be a twenty-eight year old spinster, but she wasn't without a bit of backbone.

"Heart! What a nice surprise," Mary Miller exclaimed when she opened her door. "What brings you here today?"

"My father mentioned that you had a litter of puppies. I wondered if I could see them?"

Mary's face turned into a wreath of smiles. "Yes, indeed. They're tiny now and still have their eyes closed, but Virginia knows you," she added over her shoulder as she led the way to the living room. "She won't mind you visiting."

"How many pups did she have?"

"Five!" Mary's dark brown eyes fairly glowed with happiness.

"Five puppies! That's wonderful *gut.*"

"Virginia is tired but pleased, I think."

Crouching down to the large wooden box with a blanket for Virginia and shredded paper for the pups, Heart gasped. As puppies were wont to do, they were piled all on top of each other and fast asleep. "Oh, Mary. They are adorable."

"Indeed they are." Reaching down, Mary gently rubbed the mother dog's head. "You did a good job, Virginia. It's a family to be proud of."

The *hund* thumped her tail twice, just as several puppies woke from their slumber, squeaked, and then started rooting for sustenance.

Heart sighed. "They truly are miracles, ain't so?"

"To be sure. You'll have to come back often to see how they grow."

"Are you going to keep any of them?"

"I'm afraid not. The puppies will bring me a good price. The money will be a nice addition to my savings account."

"I understand." Like Heart's father, Mary had lost her

spouse years ago. Since then she cared for elderly folks who were recovering from surgery. Heart had a feeling Mary enjoyed the job but wished it paid a bit more than it did.

Heart stayed a few more minutes, but knew it was time to go home. She was getting hungry, plus there were treats to make before her father's mysterious guest.

Just as she was about to leave, she caught sight of a cage in the corner. "What's that?"

"Hmm? Oh, that's Spike."

Heart walked closer and was startled to realize it was a pure white, rather stout rat. "Mary why do you have a rat in your living room? And why does it have a name?"

"Well, the last woman I watched passed away suddenly. She'd been a teacher or some such. This was her class's pet rat."

"I see." Of course, she didn't see at all.

Obviously reading her mind, Mary chuckled. "Spike isn't a sewer rat, he's a domesticated one."

"I didn't know there was such a thing."

"Oh, *jah*. He's smart, cuddly, and a good companion. When I realized what her awful family planned to do to him—which was chop off his head—I couldn't let him stay."

As much as Heart had never thought about keeping a rodent as a pet, she sure didn't like that idea either. "That's horrible."

"What was sad was that was the most humane way they were going to dispose of him." Her voice lowered. "He'd never done a thing to them, either. I was so upset, I took him home."

"Good for you."

"He knows his name, and when I let him out of the cage, he never goes far. Most of the time he simply crawls on my lap while I read. He really is a sweetheart." Mary sighed. "The only problem is that I don't know what I'm going to do with him now."

"You don't want a pet rat?"

"I'm going to watch another patient starting on Monday. When I broached the subject of maybe bringing Spike and keeping him in his cage in my room, everyone in my patient's family had a fit. One of the man's daughters said that he likely carried rabies."

"What are you going to do?"

"I don't know. That conversation just happened this morning."

Heart took a longer look at Spike. He stared back at her with his black eyes. A lump formed in her throat. The little rat was studying her, almost with a look of longing. He needed a home.

She certainly had that.

"I'll take him," she blurted.

Mary turned away from the rodent and gaped at her. "What?"

"I'll take Spike. I mean, if you don't mind."

"Are you sure you want him?"

"Absolutely."

"But your father. Won't Levi be upset?"

Heart was surprised that Mary knew her father's name. But that was silly. Of course she did. Apple Creek was a small community, and both of their families had lived there for some time.

Hoping she sounded more confident than she actually was, she said, "Mei father won't be upset at all. I'll keep Spike in my room. Plus, Daed is usually out in his workshop. He'll probably forget that there's even a rat living in our house." At least, she hoped that was the case. Leaning down a bit, she carefully stuck a finger through the cage and gave Spike a tiny pet.

Mary clasped her hands together. "Heart, if you could give this rat a good home, I'd be so grateful."

"Consider it done. Ah, what does Spike eat?"

Hurrying over to a cabinet in her kitchen, Mary pulled out a plastic container. "Here's all of Spike's things. He loves his chew toys and the roll of paper towels is so he can make a cozy nest." As she put all the items into a canvas bag, she added, "Rats are mighty clean, so be sure to change out the shredded paper every week. Make sure his water bottle has fresh water, too. Now, to eat, he likes rat pellets and fresh fruit and vegetables." Smiling at the little creature, Mary softened her voice. "He especially loves strawberries."

"Spike loves strawberries?"

"He enjoys being held and cuddling on your lap, too. But that might take a bit for him to warm up enough to do that."

Spike was beginning to sound far more personable-and harder to keep hidden-than she'd realized. "Okay."

Mary chuckled. "If you have questions, you know where to go. I'll help you as much as I can."

"I'll keep that in mind." Thinking of her chores and that Spike was going to need to be cared for a bit, she stood up. "I think I should probably get on my way now."

It could've been her imagination, but Mary looked rather eager for Heart to be on her way. "There's a handle at the top of his cage. It's not heavy."

Next thing Heart knew, she was headed back home with a canvas bag on her shoulder and a rat cage in her arms. She was already regretting her decision but consoled herself that a future pet sitter needed at least one pet a home.

"I hope we'll become fast friends, Spike," she muttered. "And that you'll be easy to take care of."

Unfortunately, the rat didn't squeak in reassurance. Instead, she reckoned the little guy looked rather tense and worried.

And that was all she needed to know. The little guy had lost his owner and now Mary. No doubt he was afraid she was going to be like some of the terrible relatives and murder him.

"You and I are going to get along just fine," she said. "All you have to remember is that if my daed ever does realize that you're here, he probably isn't going to be too happy about it. Don't worry, though. Although he can sound gruff, his bark is worse than his bite."

As she walked up her driveway, her heart sank. Her father was standing in front of the house talking to a young man with blond hair. Both turned to her as she approached.

Inwardly, she sighed. It seemed her father's surprise guest had arrived. And of course he was as handsome as could be.

He-and her father-were also staring at Spike's case like it was about to combust.

It seemed her secret pet rat wasn't much of a secret anymore.

Chapter 2

All things considered, Clayton's first thirty minutes with the famous Levi Beachy wasn't anything like he'd expected. Levi was known far and wide in the blacksmithing and ironworks world. Not only could he easily shoe a horse in record time, he excelled in producing true works of art. Some of the pieces he'd created had sold for thousands of dollars.

Clayton's father had given him a great deal of advice while they were waiting for an English driver to pick him up and take him to Levi's workshop. His father had cautioned him to be respectful and do his best to listen well. In addition to being a master craftsman, Levi was also known for impatience and a caustic tongue.

The man's reputation seemed to be right on the money. He was gruff, though not mean. And the projects he was working on in the back of his barn fairly took Clayton's breath away.

But then things had gotten strange real fast. After muttering something about cereal treats, Levi took him into the house.

After telling Clayton that there was no need to remove his boots, they walked inside. The first stop was the kitchen, of course.

It looked pretty much like his mother's kitchen-dishes in the sink, towels on the counter, and the makings of the mid-day meal next to the stove.

"It's ah, a right nice kitchen," he said.

"Nee, it ain't. It's a mess."

The man looked so appalled, Clayton decided he was embarrassed. "It looks fine to me. Nothing out of the ordinary."

"It's out of the ordinary for this house. And where's Heart?"

Clayton had no idea what he was talking about, so he just shrugged.

"Heart?" Levi yelled. "Heart! Where are ya?"

When almost a full moment passed, Clayton began to wonder if a comment was expected. "She doesn't seem to be here," he said at last.

Levi turned to face him. And blinked. "I think you are right. Let's go back outside."

At last he was able to put two and two together. "Your daughter's name is Heart?"

"*Jah.*"

"That is unusual."

"It is. We didn't name her that, though. Her real name is Hazel."

"Hazel. Ah."

Levi nodded. "It is a gut name. It's solid and normal." He frowned. "The girl didn't care for it much, though. Named herself Heart and there was no going back."

Given the man's forceful personality, Clayton was stunned that the girl had gotten her way. "I see."

"Ach, it is what it is, you know?" Putting both hands on his hips, he looked around the lawn. "I have to tell ya that

I'm not sure what is going on. I had really wanted those cereal treats."

Clayton wasn't sure if Levi was worried about the girl or just annoyed that she wasn't working in the kitchen. Though, she sounded like such a young, needy thing, he reckoned that his worry was probably justified.

He was just about to offer to help Levi search the grounds, when a woman appeared at the end of the driveway. As she came closer, he was aware of two things: Heart Beachy was no wayward child, not even close. Secondly, Heart was the prettiest thing he'd ever seen in his life. She had light blonde hair, a slim figure, a lovely face, and bright blue eyes. It was everything he could do not to gape.

"Is ah, that your daughter?" he asked. Just to be sure.

"*Jah.* That there is Heart." Levi frowned. "I don't know what she's carrying, though."

Realizing that the two of them were standing there staring at Heart when she could likely use a hand, Clayton started forward. "May I help ya?"

Her eyes widened. "Are you my father's guest?"

"I am. Well, I'm here because I'm Levi's new apprentice." When she continued to stare at him, he smiled slightly. "My name is Clayton. Clayton Glick. And you're Heart."

"*Jah.*"

"I'm sorry, I came out to help you yet here I am, still watching you carry the cage." He held out his hands.

"It's all right. You don't have to carry him."

"It's my pleasure." Gazing into the container, he was stunned to see a rather rotund, white rat inside. It was staring at him intently, as if it was trying to measure Clayton's worth.

It was one of the strangest things he'd ever encountered that week. Well that, and learning that Levi Beachy had a beautiful daughter who'd named herself Heart.

He gestured to the rodent. "So, what is this?"

"This is Spike."

"He looks like a rat."

"That's because he is." Her lips pressed together.

"Is he your pet?" Maybe she went for walks with the cage? It sounded unlikely, but he was beginning to think that anything was possible.

"He is now." Staring at her father, Heart released a long, drawn-out sigh. "Take Spike for me, please?" She handed him the cage and then squared her shoulders like she was walking into battle. "Let's go get this over with."

When she started forward, he fell into step beside her. When they stopped in front of Levi, Heart said, "Daed, I understand that you're gonna be having an apprentice."

"I am. It was a shame that you weren't here to greet him, though."

"I told you I was going for a walk. Remember?"

"Hmm? Oh, *jah*." He cleared his throat. "You left the kitchen a mess."

"I'll clean it in a little while."

"And there are no cereal treats."

"I'll make those, too."

Clayton hid a smile. The girl obviously had a lot of practice sparring with Levi. She didn't look cowed in the slightest.

"Father, I have a surprise for you. I now have a pet rat."

Levi's eyebrows snapped together. "You canna have them. Rats carry diseases."

"Not Spike. He's a fancy rat."

"Given the fact that he has a big cage, toys, and my new apprentice is carrying him around, I'd say that he is mite too fancy."

Heart giggled. "Fancy rats are a type of rat. Like Clydesdales are a type of horse."

"Whatever Spike is, he canna stay. I don't want to live with a rat."

"He needs a home. I want him."

"Heart-"

"Mary Miller asked us to take him, Daed."

And just like that, everything about the formidable black-smith changed. His expression softened, and his voice did too. "This rat is from Mary?"

She smiled. "It is. I'll tell you the whole story at supper." Turning to Clayton, she asked, "Will you join us for supper?"

Without taking the time to check with Levi, Clayton nodded. "I would love to join you. Danke."

Her soft smile transformed into a bright grin. "You're welcome. It's the least I could do, given that you're carrying around my pet rat and all. Will you bring him inside for me?"

"*Jah*, sure." After he took two steps, he looked back at Levi. The man hadn't moved from where he was standing. His arms were folded across his chest, and he looked mighty perplexed. "I'll be right back out, Levi."

"Take your time," he said as he started walking toward the barn. "I, uh, have something I need to take care of anyway."

When the man was out of sight, Heart chuckled. "Don't fret, Clayton. My father wanders off all the time. You'll get used to it. Now, let's go inside and see what Spike thinks of his new home."

Clayton followed her to the house. He was no rat, but if he had to guess, he'd reckon that the animal was going to like his new home just fine.

He certainly did.